Educational Luminaries

Triumphing Over Systemic Hurdles

Donna Vallese, Ph.D, Founder of Inspiring Leaders
María Angélica Benavides, Ed.D, B-Global
Publisher
Dr. Randi D. Ward, Editor

Donna Vallese, Ph.D • María Angélica Benavides, Ed.D
Luca Ceccarelli • Yesenia Reinoso • Aaron Robbins • Lisa Polk
Louise Debreczeny • Dr. Beverly Knox-Pipes • Victoria Schulman
Dr. Jerri-Lynn Williams-Harper • Elizabeth Power
Sylvia Badwi • Nebiyou Timotewos

**Educational Luminaries:
Triumphing Over Systemic Hurdles**

**Published by B-Global Publishing
Copyright © 2024**

ISBN: 978-1-963980-09-7

Dedication

This book is dedicated to the countless students and adults who have felt lost, left behind, or defeated by the very system meant to empower them. To those who struggled in school, who felt that the classroom was not a place for them, who felt like failures when they stumbled or fell short, we see you. We acknowledge your experiences, and we deeply apologize for the times when the system seemed to fail you.

You are valuable, and your potential is boundless. Your journey matters, and your voice deserves to be heard. This book was written with you in mind, with the hope of bridging the gap that so often leaves individuals feeling isolated and unsupported. We believe that learning should inspire, uplift, and ignite curiosity—not extinguish it.

May this book serve as a step toward creating an educational system that lifts every learner, recognizes every story, and ignites a love of learning in all. We honor your resilience, your spirit, and your determination, and we are committed to helping build a future where education embraces everyone.

Acknowledgment

We would like to extend our heartfelt gratitude to all the previous authors who contributed to the *Educational Matadores* series. Your dedication and insights have laid the foundation for the transformative ideas presented in this new work, and your passion for education continues to inspire us.

In *The Educational Luminaries,* we are honored to recognize and acknowledge a new generation of visionaries—our education luminaries. These courageous individuals have shared their voices, ideas, and innovations, daring to bring forth powerful perspectives that challenge and enrich the educational system. Your contributions are a beacon of hope and change, lighting the way for future generations of learners and leaders.

To all the teachers and leaders who dedicate themselves tirelessly to the growth and well-being of students, we honor you. Your unwavering commitment, compassion, and resilience bring light into classrooms and hearts alike. You educate, guide, motivate, and inspire young minds to persevere and dream, even when the path seems challenging. It is through your work that the next generation finds the strength to move forward, and we are grateful for the profound impact you have on countless lives.

Thank you for all that you do, for your courage, and for your relentless pursuit of a brighter future in education. May this book serve as a testament to your influence and a source of inspiration as we continue to elevate and evolve the educational experience for all.

TABLE OF CONTENTS

Foreword
By: Dr.Jaya Sajnani

In a world where education is evolving to meet the demands of an interconnected, rapidly changing society, *The Educational Luminaries* offers a beacon of inspiration and transformation. This book isn't just a collection of theories and practices; it's a roadmap for reimagining what education can be. Through groundbreaking insights from educators and thought leaders across disciplines, it bridges gaps that traditional systems have left unaddressed, pushing boundaries and exploring new pathways for learning.

The vision shared in this book resonates deeply with my life's work and values. As the Founder and Chief Executive of YG Travel and Helping Hand Foundation in the UK, and through my role with Global Talent Solution, I have witnessed firsthand the profound impact that access to quality education and support can have on young minds. I believe education should not only inform but also inspire and empower. This book reflects that vision, presenting ideas that promise to make learning a transformative experience for every student, regardless of background.

The contributors to The Educational Luminaries are not merely educators; they are pioneers who understand that education must be inclusive, holistic, and forward-thinking. From addressing trauma in the classroom to harnessing artificial intelligence and fostering media literacy, these experts provide readers with insights that are as practical as they are visionary. Their contributions illuminate a future where educational institutions do more than prepare students for exams—they prepare them for life, resilience, and leadership in a complex world.

It is my hope that as you delve into these chapters, you will find not only knowledge but also the courage to challenge and expand our conventional educational frameworks. Let this book be a catalyst for change in classrooms, communities, and beyond.

Dr. Jaya Sajnani

Founder and Chief Executive, YG Travel, Helping Hand Foundation,
UK and Global Talent Solution UK Chairperson, LOANI Global UK,
UK Director of GSFE
jsajnani@globaltalentsolutionhub.com
www.globaltalentsolutionhub.com
+447808522157

Preface
Matadores to Luminaries – A New Vision for Education
By: Dr. Angelica Benavides

As we embark on this journey within *The Educational Luminaries*, it is essential to share why we have chosen to evolve from *Educational Matadores* to *Educational Luminaries*. This shift is more than just a change in name; it is a reflection of our deepened commitment and expanded vision for education.

In our early days as the *Educational Matadores*, our focus was on challenging conventional thinking, breaking down barriers, and pushing through the obstacles within the educational system—much like matadores in an arena. We recognized that education was a space where courage and resilience were required to navigate complex challenges. We have honored and celebrated the fierce determination of educators, students, and leaders striving for excellence within traditional structures.

However, as the needs of our communities and students evolved, so did our perspective. We recognized the growing importance of fostering light, inspiration, and guidance within education. Our mission expanded beyond overcoming obstacles to illuminating pathways, nurturing innovation, and shining a beacon of hope and possibility for all. Thus, *Educational Luminaries* was born—a name that captures our commitment to lighting the way forward for the next generation of learners and leaders.

As luminaries, we are focused on creating spaces that inspire growth, illuminate new ideas, and foster a collaborative spirit that transcends barriers. This book represents our dedication to introducing fresh perspectives, diverse voices, and groundbreaking practices into education, moving us closer to an inclusive, innovative system that values every learner.

Our goal is clear: to empower a generation of educators, leaders, and students who see themselves as changemakers capable of shaping a brighter, more inclusive future.

Living Through Cultural Responsivity
By: Dr. Donna Vallese

Imagine my excitement last year when we were just about to publish *Ed. Matadores: Revolutionizing the Educational System.* It was the beginning of a movement to really start to make important shifts in the educational system. I have worked with hundreds of educators in many capacities throughout my career and have developed a core group of colleagues who were excited to see a new approach to informing change.

Just before the launch, though, my bubble deflated when an old college friend, also an educator, bravely reached out to tell me that although she loved the idea of what we were trying to do with the book and wanted to be an author in it, as a member of the Latino community she could not participate. She was grappling with the title and its representation of historical colonization. I was stunned and confused at the same time… we had vetted this title to so many people, and in fact, our publisher, Dr. Angelica Benevides, and one other author who was also from the Latino community—had not expressed any concerns with it. However, as the discussion continued, I began to understand her perspective. While our book approached the title through a lens of ending practices that were ineffective in helping students, from her perspective, violence, and harm were at the forefront of the title. For us, the title symbolized a shift away from outdated and unproductive educational methods that may have perpetuated inequity rather than any association with historical acts of colonization.

Her interpretation underscored an essential point about the significance of language in education reform: it should evoke progress, empowerment, and the dismantling of ineffective practices, without unintentionally invoking the trauma of historical oppression.

So, we started an inquiry to understand the issue of our title better.

My college friend, Alexandra Lopez, and I had a long exchange of messages, and ultimately, the challenge for her was in the term matador, which means killer or murderer in Spanish and has strong ties to the conquistadores that had negatively impacted her culture throughout history. I explained to her that had never crossed my mind and that we had been inspired by the song *Matador* by Los Fabulosos Cadillacs, which described a man in hiding from the government who was hunting him down because he was outspoken about social injustices. We saw matadores as people who were going to transform the educational system. She understood that, but it still did not change how she felt about the terminology we had chosen for the title.

I have gone through dozens of hours in culturally responsive and bias training prior to this, and I even coach leaders in diversity, equity, and inclusion. I am an active partner for underrepresented populations. How could I have missed this? I lost sleep over it, talked to my partner at length about it, talked to the editor, Angelica Benevides, about it, researched conquistadores, and reached out to Latino colleagues and friends as well as those from other underrepresented populations. My colleagues and friends helped me gain clarity and understanding of the situation.

How could I make this right? It was too late to change the title of this particular book. We were ready to publish. It was too late for this first book, but I knew that in the next book, we could and should manage a title change to the brand. Dr. Angelica and I decided that who better to ask than our authors who participated in the book to help us determine the next direction for this movement?

In December 2023, we held a live event with the authors of Ed. Matadores for a book signing and to give them a speaking platform. Prior to the event, we held a mastermind where we could help each other out with pressing problems. Dr. Angelica and I started the conversation with the authors about the title of the next book.

Together, we sat in the wide-open lobby of the beautiful Hotel Syracuse and had a deep and honest discourse about the title of our book. It turned out that the title bothered some of the authors but they still chose to participate because the cause was much greater than the title. Some authors felt that we should just continue with the existing title because of the intent behind it. Some felt that we shouldn't change just because of a few, while others felt we should change to ensure inclusivity. We spent far longer discussing this issue than any of us anticipated, but the group of authors truly wanted to help us find the best path forward. By the end of our mastermind time, we had decided the following:

- *If we are promoting change to ensure equity, we must do everything we can to ensure everyone has a voice.*

- *If we are to say that we are culturally responsive, we need to model it.*

- *If we are promoting change, we must demonstrate that we can pivot if we expect others in our field to do the same, even if it seems hard.*

- *If we believe in our mission to transform the educational system, our message will always be stronger than any title.*

- *When we know better, we must do better (just like Maya Angelou suggested).*

So, here we are... our second book - *Educational Luminaries.* Dr. Angelica and I resorted to an AI tool to help us brainstorm a long list of possibilities. We were struck by the word "luminary" because of the dual meaning of giving or shedding light onto something as well as someone who inspires or influences. We know our educational system needs some drastic changes to ensure that every learner has access to an education that is meaningful, engaging, and equitable. Educational Luminaries will always seek to bring solutions to the biggest challenges that hinder learning for many students.

Educational Luminaries: Triumphing Over Systemic Hurdles

Thank you Alexsandra, for your courage to help lead us to this new title that we believe is far better than our original one. May we all continue to light the path to a better, more inclusive and equitable future!

The Courage to Speak Up
By: Alexsandra López, Ms Ed, CCC Bilingual SLP

In June 2023, I received an email from my college friend, Dr. Donna Vallese, announcing a collaborative educational reform initiative. I was intrigued as this aligned with the ethos of my work offering love, equity, inclusion and care for all and centering our students. I then read the title, "Ed Matadores." My reaction was a deeply visceral one. Language matters. English in the United States is imbued with violent idioms used on a daily basis. Normalizing violent language is a step away from physical violence.

The title prompted a flashback to attending a bullfight in Spain in 1993 at 16 years old. Before attending, I learned about this tradition in books and through what my white American Spanish teacher described as a quintessential cultural experience. In pictures, I saw bullfighters dressed in ornate costumes waving red capes. The bullfighter stabs the bull with *banderillas* and wooden lance spikes with colorful ends, as the objective of a bullfight is to kill the bull. The pictures romanticized this long-standing tradition of colonial violence.

My young self was not prepared for what I would see. The still pictures in the encyclopedia did not do justice to the palpable feeling in the stadium. I was confused by seeing a crowd unified in validating colonial violence. My face was buried in my hands for most of the event. I peeked through my fingers when the crowd cheered so loudly it was deafening. That is when I saw a moment of sheer horror etched in my brain forever. The crowd was on their feet, cheering as the first lance was thrust into the bull as he ran away. I could see and sense the bull's pain accompanied by a visceral gut-punch feeling. Each swell of the crowd noise correlated with another thrust of a new lance as the bull was slowly and painfully killed.

The bullfight was my first experience with the colonial arm of my identity as Puerto Rican with Spanish, African, and Indigenous blood. *Matador*, in Spanish, means "killer"... I was confused about how my white Spanish teacher felt this violence was a "quintessential experience" for me.

The title also made me think of my experience attending school in a small rural school district in Western New York. I spent my childhood leaning into whiteness to hide my multiple marginalized identities, especially being Puerto Rican and a native Spanish speaker. I hid my authentic self to blend in with my white peers due to daily microaggressions, racial gaslighting (from peers and staff), and racial bullying from peers that began verbally when I was 3 years old and escalated into unprompted racial and physical violence against me in elementary and middle school. I leaned into looking, acting, and speaking "white" for safety. From a young age, I was aware I could never bring my full self to school due to this spirit murdering.

My financially comfortable peers were akin to the *matador* in ornate clothing as they lunged lances, through words and fists, at me. The school staff were the roaring crowd by engaging in or inadvertently encouraging these actions and failing to come to my defense. I remember after an instance of physical violence, walking down the hallway at the end of the school day, bleeding from my eyes, not being able to see while **so** many people saw me. With a visceral feeling in my stomach, my only thought was that my mom would not be able to get me. How would I get home? I stumbled into the middle school office, bloody tears rolling down my face to speak to the secretary. It was obvious something terrible had happened, yet she had not asked me anything. I was afraid to get in trouble or get anyone else in trouble despite just being brazenly attacked. The primary attacker had two accomplices, one held my hands, the other my feet, while she hit my face. She was throwing her lances while the other two girls were cheering her on. I then thought about the *querencia*, a sanctuary in a person or place where one feels a sense of love and safety; in bullfighting, this is the space in the ring where the bull goes to feel safe and gather strength. The bull is futilely seeking sanctuary but unquestionably is not safe or feels love.

I ruminated about the email from Donna with that familiar visceral feeling for hours. I was confused. How was this analogy linked to colonial violence and murder going to serve students? Due to their violent and cruel nature, several countries that held bullfights no longer do so, and animal rights groups have elevated this message. I was further confused upon seeing that Donna's co-author was Latina. I then thought about what I would share as a facilitator, coach, or thought partner if this scenario were brought to me.

First and foremost, we are all learning, and simultaneously intent doesn't equal impact. As a facilitator, I would open the space with both a joke and a reminder that we are going to misstep, as we should! The critical step is care work, which happens after the moment we stumble. Do we then listen to understand or just to respond? Do we engage in *re*flection or in *de*flection?

Marginalized, minoritized, and historically underserved people are rarely offered a seat at the table,. So often, if there is *a* representative from a marginalized group, it is felt there is *adequate* representation. No group is a monolith, regardless of ethnicity and/or identity. Due to the power imbalance, persons of color may not feel comfortable speaking up. It is common in spaces to *say* there is a belief in equitable practices. Equity is an action to embody. Unfortunately, most efforts are lip service and performative in nature, only serving to maintain the status quo.

I realized I had to say something to Donna, but how? My formative years had been spent hiding my identities while simultaneously being thrust into a role as an advocate for my two young Spanish-speaking disabled cousins, Stephanie and Arnold, who are now my ancestors. Given the inequitable and racist treatment that I witnessed them receive and I also received, I could no longer be silent as a moral obligation. My "why" was to create the teacher I needed as a young English Language Learner (ELL). Simultaneously, channeling that visceral feeling to fuel my advocacy, turning my pain to purpose as a love letter to them to serve all children.

Donna and I had never had a conversation such as this. The usual fearful questions came to mind:
- How do I approach this from a "call in" vs. "call" out perspective
- How do I keep myself regulated, heart-centered, and open to what is said?
- What if what I offer is not heard?
- What if the person doesn't like me or I lose this friendship?
- What if I say something that causes harm?

With a lump in my throat and stomach, I reached out to my college friend. I was pleasantly surprised by the dialogue and response. It solidified my experiences that those who want to engage in the work, will. This was not easy. It would have been very easy for the authors to keep the name as time, effort, marketing, and branding were already in place. They could also have chosen to appease those in the group who felt the name should remain, feeling that the mission was more important than the name.

I want to amplify that when Donna made this decision, she shared that she planned to give me credit. Upon hearing this, my heart swelled. For non-BILAPOC (Black, Indigenous, Latin, Asian, and People Of Color), this may seem like common practice. As a woman of color, it is very common not to receive credit. I have had my words and ideas stated verbatim by others without credit for years. Yet I saw these same colleagues credit their fellow white colleagues, and I always credited my colleagues. In these instances, I again felt the visceral gut punch. I decided to settle in the fact that my words had an impact and were being shared to create an impact for children.

As I sat to write this response, I had not fully contemplated how the gut punch was a thematic thread for me as a learner and educator. Each time I somatically experienced this sensation in my body, it always derived from an outside source.

I realized when I saw the term *matadores* being used in an educational context, it was aligned to my harm as a student and an educator, which is the experience for many educators of color. I realized when I read that email I was being catapulted to the moment I saw, experienced, and *felt* the bullfight. I felt like the lances being put into the bull were being put into *me*. That is not an experience I would want for children as we work collaboratively to build a more inclusive and supportive educational system.

As Rumi offered, "Yesterday I was clever, so I wanted to change the world. Today I am wise, so I am changing myself." Each of us has the ability to engage in individual change. In daily interactions with students, we may cause unintentional harm. How can a child use their voice if they do not feel valued? This conditioning continues in the form of microaggressions, and marginalized children grow up thinking they do not have a voice. It also may manifest in thinking that names for people, and in this case for a cause, is not of vital importance.

I am very grateful to Donna for being open and making space in her mind and, most importantly, in her heart for this conversation. BILAPOC communities have been elevating this conversation, but unfortunately, unless it is rubberstamped by non-BILAPOC communities, It is not validated. Donna's open-heartedness is an example of what being open to courageous conversation and moving into a brave space can look like. Authentically engaging in this space is the true meaning of *querencia:* love and safety for ourselves, our communities, and our children.

Introduction

In today's rapidly evolving world, education must be more than just the transmission of knowledge; it must be a bridge to understanding, innovation, and profound personal and societal transformation. *Educational Luminaries: Triumphing Over Systemic Hurdles* brings together a collective of visionary educators and trailblazers from diverse industries, each contributing unique perspectives and strategies to reshape the future of learning in meaningful ways.

The origins of this book and its authors are rooted in a shared mission to address the critical needs within our educational system. Dr. Angelica Benavides, a retired Special Education Director turned publisher, and Dr. Donna met serendipitously in April of 2022 at Crom Castle in Northern Ireland. In this historic setting, surrounded by the legacy of resilience and innovation, two passionate advocates for education reform connected over their mutual concerns about the deep inequities and systemic inadequacies that continue to challenge our educational landscape. From the outset, we knew that our work together would be necessary to create meaningful change.

Over the following months, our commitment to education reform only grew stronger. In countless conference calls between New York and Texas, we reflected on the well-meaning but ultimately unsuccessful attempts we had witnessed in trying to "fix" education. While there were inspiring examples of innovation and change in certain places, none seemed to create the deep, systemic impact needed to truly transform education. This realization brought urgency to our conversations, reminding us that real change would require more than isolated initiatives—it would demand a collective movement of dedicated leaders.

As we brainstormed and problem-solved, we were inspired by our experiences in professional networking events, including the one that had brought us together in the unlikely setting of a castle. There was something about the synergy created by gathering like-minded individuals who genuinely cared about making the world better.

It was in these reflections that *Educational Matadores* was born, with a vision of sharing transformative narratives of educational leaders and building a united community focused on revolutionizing education.

As this idea evolved, *Educational Luminaries* emerged as a more fitting representation of our mission. Together, we saw the potential of connecting extraordinary leaders, educators, and innovators—individuals who had also felt the weight of systemic hurdles yet remained undeterred in their commitment to impact. This movement would highlight their stories and empower them to collaborate, ultimately driving real change within the educational system. We envisioned a series of books, each a testament to the courage, vision, and dedication of these pioneers, building a powerful grassroots movement of changemakers united in purpose and equipped to transform education from the ground up.

The Educational Luminaries serves as a platform for these pioneering voices—leaders in fields as varied as diversity, trauma, technology, and media literacy—who introduce concepts and approaches that may be new to educators and educational leaders. These luminaries have not only identified crucial gaps in traditional education but also present transformative insights and tools designed to equip educators, students, and communities with the resources needed for a dynamic, inclusive, and impactful educational experience.

Through each chapter, readers are invited to explore innovative practices that challenge conventional systems and policies, encouraging us to view education through new lenses and embrace interdisciplinary approaches. Together, we are on a mission to prepare today's learners for the challenges of tomorrow by equipping current and future educators with groundbreaking ideas, methods, and visions that foster resilience, empathy, and creativity.

Ultimately, *The Educational Luminaries* seeks to inspire a collective revolution in education—one that integrates new fields, ideas, and methods, bridging divides to create a forward-thinking, inclusive educational system. This book is a call to action for those who believe in the transformative power of learning and are committed to creating an educational landscape that truly serves all. With this book as our guide, we are sparking a movement that empowers educators, motivates students, and connects communities, paving the way for a brighter, more connected future.

ARTIFICIAL INTELLIGENCE AND THE GREAT PEDAGOGICAL PARADIGM SHIFT

By: Luca Ceccarelli

aiSynergy Leadership Development
An AI Literacy & Leadership Company

The Rise of *GenAI Natives*

History will characterize the 2020s as the dawn of the Age of Artificial Intelligence. Although AI development began in the 1940s, the rapid advancements since 2023 have brought AI into the mainstream. Tension rises as AI weaves its way into every sector of daily life, education included. As humanity grapples with the implications of AI cascading into the very fabric of society, a series of questions emerge: What role does AI have in the classroom? How will students and educators use it? What are best practices? Can AI bridge learning gaps? And what is *'AI Privilege'*—the advantages granted by access to AI tools? *GenAI Natives* will soon enter the workforce, where AI mastery will give them critical advantages. Now is the time to help them hone their prowess and adopt AI responsibly. While we will not focus on regulatory debates or the broader societal implications of AI, this chapter addresses the stigma of using AI by encouraging responsible adoption and offers best practices, frameworks, and additional resources for future reference.

We are far away from *The Singularity*—the moment when technology enters a perpetual cycle of its own design and self-improvement. For the foundations of our exploration today, we will look at AI for what it currently is: an accelerated knowledge-base aggregator with limitations, boundaries, and parameters, completely reliant on large data-sets. While current iterations of Generative AI can categorize knowledge with mind-boggling speed, accuracy, and uncanny human-like affect, it lacks critical reasoning and human emotions, pivotal axioms to cognition and morality.

AI is neither our friend nor enemy. It's not always right (actually, it's often wrong). Therefore, one needs to consistently apply critical thinking to its responses.

It's evident that AI can very easily be harnessed by the dark side, to cheat, do homework, and even unleash considerable suffering, including AI-assisted bullying—a growing concern we explore in-depth through resources at aiSynergy. For now, however, let's posit or assume AI as a tool for the greater good, expertly curated with a benevolent moral code. In truth, youth around the world are surrounded by contradictory values, exacerbated by environmental, industrial, social, and political alarm. Many young people are understandably overwhelmed by the state of the world, exhibiting symptoms of anxiety, apathy, self-harm, and worse. Here, AI can offer hope. It's solution-oriented by design, and in the classroom, it can empower students to streamline their learning, assist with research, and even help them tackle real-world problems. This is the revolution AI brings: an opportunity for students to "be the change *they* wish to see in the world".

Prove vs Improve AI Ethos™

The core of AI usage in education should be grounded in trust and integrity. To address the stigma surrounding AI, we must shift the focus from seeing it as a shortcut to recognizing it as a powerful tool for growth. Akin to any "shadow behavior", when the stigma is relieved, so is its power. This leads us to the *Prove vs Improve AI Ethos*™.

> *Am I using AI to PROVE that I know something I don't know, or am I using it to IMPROVE something I'm developing?*

The concept takes root in various psychological and educational theories. Influenced by contributors like Carol Dweck's research on fixed and growth mindsets (Dweck, 2006), John Dewey's emphasis on experiential learning (Dewey, 1938, 1986), and humanistic psychology's focus on personal growth, this framework encourages individuals to shift their perspective from *proving* their abilities to focusing on continuous *improvement* and learning. Every time someone uses AI they must ask themselves this fundamental question.

Personal development is key. As long as students are using AI to enhance their learning, they are growing. The moment they resort to shortcuts, everyone loses. Teachers should avoid getting trapped in the inescapable web of verification or attempts to catch cheaters—who will always exist. AI will continue to evolve, making detection software unreliable, and students will get better at making AI adopt their voice. Instead, we must encourage students to be responsible for their own AI usage, focusing on leadership, growth, and integrity. When students do their own work, there's a sense of pride. Pointing to the question of if they feel that their efforts are "theirs", and if it is helping them improve rather than prove, will help reinforce this.

Philanthropic AI™

Unleashing the power of AI can fuel creativity, engagement, and impact. To harness this potential, we developed an off-the-shelf program catering to high-school students who want to boost their profile for their college applications, *Philanthropic AI*™. Admissions staff are keen to see demonstrations of character and how students engage with their community, pursue their interests, and distinguish themselves beyond mere GPA and test scores. For many students, this can be a daunting and even deflating mission. *Philanthropic AI* was designed as a transformative, educational, and interactive program to empower students with practical applications of AI for personal growth and community impact. The program combines learning and applying AI with a focus on character enrichment and social responsibility. Students are guided through the basics of prompt engineering, enabling them to research, create, and implement a purposeful community outreach plan that aligns with their own interests—and looks great on college applications.

Past projects have included enabling access to educational resources and games, creating self-growth and introspection platforms, engaging in community projects, and accessing mental health resources; all of them revolved around using AI for the greater good. More details, examples and teacher toolkits may be found at aiSynergy.net.

AI at FACE Value™ – Best Practices for Students Using AI

Let's take a closer look at some frameworks to help introduce AI in the classroom. The first building block to accessing the benefits of AI is to understand *AI at FACE Value*. The acronym F.A.C.E. points to a comprehensive bird's-eye view for framing AI: Fundamentals, Applications, Challenges, and Ethics. **Fundamentals** include AI history, basic definitions, and how and where AI sources information, etc.

Applications involves understanding distinctions between models like LLM, NLP, and Generative, how they're already being used (often in common applications that users are unaware are using AI, such as Siri/Alexa, music playlists, social ads, Grammarly, navigation, etc), and Generative AI platforms (like producing complex text, images, videos, etc.). **Challenges** speak to understanding limitations, bias, privacy concerns, AI dependence, incorrect answers, and "hallucinations". Finally, **Ethics** involves more philosophical discussions on if, how, when, and why AI should be used, and the greater implications to society. We have found that these ethical considerations tend to stimulate dynamic classroom discussions with opportunities for games and reflection that urge students to evaluate this pivotal moment in human history. Students often comment that they loved these activities and that they sparked their thinking about social evolution and AI's role, so we've made the content and instructions available for educators to easily access and download.

The SMART Prompt

Effective AI use starts with understanding the prompt—a user's question or statement that guides AI's response. The art of prompt engineering is critical to crafting clear queries that yield desired results. This is where *The SMART Prompt* comes in— creating prompts that are Specific, Measurable, Achievable, Relevant, and *Task-oriented (variation on

Doran, 1981). **The *SMART Prompt*** encourages users to engage with AI in a manner that is thoughtful and purposeful, thereby enhancing the quality of conversation and output. Note that we have altered the classic final Doran SMART Goal from "Time-bound" to *Task-oriented. AI always works best when given a specific task.

Examples of simple prompts (which will yield vague results):
A)   "Tell me about climate change."
B)   "I'm looking for a cool robotics project for my class."

Examples rewritten as a *SMART Prompt:*

A)   Prompt: "Provide a detailed summary of the most recent research available to you on the effects of climate change on ocean health, acidification, and temperature increases. Highlight key findings and any notable trends or changes. Include sources."

SMART: This prompt is specific (detailed summary of the most recent research—available to the AI platform), measurable (clear focus on 'key findings' and 'trends' with attention to citing sources), achievable (clearly defined parameters - ocean health, acidification, and temperature increases), relevant (current environmental issue), and task-oriented (AI is to provide a 'detailed summary').

B)   Prompt: "Create a few options for a six-month personal development plan for a high school student interested in task-oriented robotics, including monthly goals, resources needed, and key skills to be developed."

SMART: It's specific (requesting a plan for task-oriented robotics interest), asking for a series of options providing alternatives and options for the author to evaluate (measurable), focuses on realistic goal-setting (achievable), aligns with specific student interests and required resources (relevant), and specifies the task for the AI (a 'few options for a 6-month plan').

The AI CAVE™ – Best Practices for Students Using AI

One of the more contentious aspects of students using AI in their schoolwork is how teachers will recognize its use. While this ultimately boils down to leadership and integrity, we've developed a set of best practices that are most effective when adopted school-wide. Engaging an external consultant can greatly support this kind of change management, ensuring a smooth and cohesive transition. These foundational guidelines are rooted in what we call *'The AI CAVE.'*

- **Cite AI**: Students should cite how they used AI. What was the prompt they used? Which AI platform? Why did they elect to use AI? *Teachers and principals should evaluate and implement the approach that works best for their institutional culture, reflecting how circumstantial and detailed they want citations to be.
- **Accuracy and Actuality**: AI platforms vary in internet connectivity. While students believe they are accessing current information, a lot of it might be outdated. As we know, just because it's on the internet that doesn't make it true.
- **Verification and Critical Thinking**: AI often provides inaccurate or fabricated information. Students must verify accuracy and cite primary sources (or practices in keeping with the school's approach to sources). AI might be a stepping stone to this ultimate goal, but the direct information that it provides is not.
- **Ethical Use**: AI blurs the lines between creativity, effort, and assistance. Students need to consider the ethical implications of using AI in contexts where originality, independent thinking, or the struggle to articulate one's ideas are integral to the task at hand.

AI is a much better research partner and editor than it is an "author".

Conclusion

In this chapter, we have introduced a few basic AI concepts, including more sophisticated ways of tasking AI. By embracing frameworks like *Prove vs Improve AI Ethos*™, *AI at FACE Value*™, *The SMART Prompt*, and *The AI CAVE*™ *~ Best Practices for Students Using AI,* we can guide students toward responsible AI use that fosters creativity, critical thinking, and ethical problem-solving. *Philanthropic AI* is one such example of how students can use AI to develop not only their intellect and learn applicable life skills but also enrich their character and use AI for the greater good. These are all skills that will not only distinguish them in their academic careers but will also shape the future of a society increasingly interwoven with artificial intelligence.

We encourage you to take a look at our website to explore more resources, develop your toolkits, and join the conversation.

aiSynergy.net

References

Dewey, J. (1938, 1986). *Experience and education. In The educational forum* (Vol. 50, No. 3). Taylor & Francis Group.

Doran, G. T. (1981). *There's a S.M.A.R.T. Way to Write Management's Goals and Objectives* (70th ed., Vol. 35-36). Journal of Management Review.

Dweck, C. S. (2006). *Mindset: The New Psychology of Success.* Random House Publishing Group.

AI Usage in this Chapter

How was AI used for this work? AI did not generate any of the concepts, nor did it write any of the content. However, the author sought assistance with wordsmithing a few sentences which were proving long-winded or vague.

Google Gemini was used to help find and identify citations.
ChatGPT4 and GPT4o was used to analyze paragraphs for internal discussion and comment, much like one might look for a peer review or editorial considerations.

Conclusion: inasmuch as the author had presented all original concepts and did not have AI write the content, the following prompt was used to generate the first draft of the conclusion:

Prompt: ... *While maintaining my writing style, can you write a draft for a potential conclusion to the chapter?* ChatGPT did an impressive job at this task, however the content was not used for word economy.

Finally, AI was tasked with reducing the overall word count of the chapter—as it is part of a larger body of work and needed to be reduced by about 70%. Unfortunately various AI platforms proved unsuccessful at this task, generating dry, highly abbreviated content (at the expense of author's voice and conceptual integrity); generating confusing and misleading results... so ultimately old fashioned editing was required for this task. As noted in the body of the chapter: *AI is a much better research partner and editor than it is an "author".*

In Greek mythology, Talos, a bronze giant crafted by Hephaestus, was gifted to King Minos, and served as Crete's protector. Patrolling the island's shores, the robot hurled boulders at approaching ships and could heat its body to destroy enemies with its fiery embrace. A first known example of conceptual AI? - Image by Dall•e

Get to Know Luca

In 2023 Luca founded aiSynergy.net, an AI literacy and leadership consultancy helping students, educators, and home schools navigate the crossroads of education and AI by empowering ethical and thoughtful integration for the collective betterment of humanity. Born in England and raised in Rome, Italy, Luca lives in Santa, New Mexico.

Author Note:

aiSynergy Leadership is a Subsidiary of HDNM Consulting, inc.
aiSynergy.net | HDNM.com
Correspondence concerning this chapter should be addressed to Luca
Ceccarelli: LucaConsults@HDNM.com
825 Calle Mejia #334, Santa Fe, NM 87501

BRIDGING THE GAP: RE-INTEGRATING MEDIA LITERACY INTO PUBLIC EDUCATION

By: Yesenia Reinoso

Photo Credit: Illinois Civics Hub. (2023, September 15). Media Literacy Toolkit. Illinois Civics Hub. https://www.illinoiscivics.org/standards/media-literacy-toolkit/.

"Media literacy is not just important; it's absolutely critical. It's going to make the difference between whether kids are a tool of the mass media or whether the mass media is a tool for kids to use," (Ellerbee, 2009).

Since the beginning of time, media and education have had a unique connection. Through traditional and now digital media channels, students can access any information with their fingertips. In today's landscape, it is oversaturated, and the youth live in a world of potent 24/7, 365-day media. It is everywhere, and now, combined with technology, it is embedded into everyday life. Everybody consumes media online and lives in a household with more than one electronic device.

Media: The Key to Global Communication

As someone from the communications world, I understand just how potent media can be. Communication is the primary source of information. I may come from a different area of education – the corporate world rather than academic – but my role as a communicator is also that of an educator.

As Founder and Principal of Y Communicate, I focus on helping clients find their way through storytelling and informing the public about what's happening inside and outside their business. The power of transparent information helps humans transform into decisive thinkers and innovative producers.

The mission of Ed Luminaries is to overhaul and transform the educational system with new innovative initiatives to put students in positions to succeed. Today, the education system must prepare students for the arduous job market and have academics aligned with the skills needed by the youth. In addition, young people should also reacquaint themselves with civics, finance, and home economics. Outdated policies, underfunded schools, and lack of teacher support are the primary reasons the U.S. education system needs to be revised (Benevides, 2023). It is why organizations such as Ed Luminaries must lead in the renaissance of the U.S. education system.

The Need to Shape Media Literacy

From an academic standpoint, media literacy equips students with the necessary techniques and information to critically analyze, evaluate, and develop media across numerous mediums. Students understand the power of media and how messaging can instantly impact their mindsets. Even more noteworthy is that with the increased screen time, the children can quickly engage in any subject and become empowered. Today's youth, 92% to be exact, according to National Association for Media Literacy Education (NAMLE) (2023), are online every day.

Just as children need to know the basics of mathematics, history, science, and reading, the same can be said about media literacy. Students heavily rely on academia to craft their media competence, empowering them with the skills to navigate the complex and diverse messaging of today's world (Media Literacy Now, 2024).

Media literacy is a life skill. In many ways, it should already be incorporated into the curriculum at all grade levels. However, it is not. The reasons include inadequate resources, a lack of funding, outdated educational training, and insufficient advocacy for supportive legislation.

With the overwhelming amount of misinformation and disinformation, it is becoming more difficult for youth to combat and decipher truth from fiction accurately. In corporate communications, our role as communicators can shapeshift how the public consumes information, how it is given, and why people should invest in it. Communication professionals are like teachers, educating and informing the public about any topic that appeals to them.

The intersectionality between corporate communications and academia cannot be overstated. There are parallels in how we inform and educate people, and we cannot deny the soft power it brings when assessing influence.

Media Literacy: Enhancing Critical Thinking and Communication Across All Media and Ages

Before we continue, let's first understand the basic definition of media literacy. According to Dictionary.com, media literacy is the ability to critically analyze the content created and consumed in various media, including radio and television, the internet, and social media, for accuracy, credibility, or evidence of bias (Dictionary.com, 2024).

According to the National Association for Media Literacy Education (2023), the primary functions of media literacy are access, analysis, evaluation, creation, and action. In education, media literacy empowers individuals to navigate the ever-changing landscape of news and communications.

To maneuver through media effectively, students must acquire critical thinking skills to ask essential questions, evaluate information, avoid manipulation, and openly engage in traditional or digital spaces. Teachers must teach those skill sets at the elementary school level.

According to Media Literacy Now (2024), the organization expressed the following points:

- Skills that magnify the concept of literacy must be taught in various formats rather than simply reading or writing. Today's messaging is complex and diverse.

- When focusing on a specific issue, use techniques and critical thinking to study the problems and generate tangible solutions to combat the negative messages.
- We are developing critical thinking capabilities to empower everyone to participate in society worldwide.

Photo Credit: Franziska Barczyk for NPR. Carrillo, S. (2023, November 8). Like it or not: Kids hear the news. Here's how teachers help them understand it. NPR.

Fundamental concepts about the different media types and methods to distinguish facts in storytelling are introduced at the elementary level. Implementing media literacy involves adding age-appropriate activities for students to explore and analyze. This stage is where critical thinking skills commence as children question the content consumed, understand key storytelling elements, and recognize the basic persuasive practices.

Early exposure to media literacy sets the foundation for students to become well-rounded individuals as they grow up. It fosters curiosity, inspires inquiry-based lessons, and endorses responsible digital citizenship.

In middle school, media literacy education expands to introduce complex topics, including media bias, social media influences and behavioral characteristics, and audience targeting. Recent research suggests adolescents over twelve spend approximately nine hours a day consuming media, which has positive and negative effects. The adolescent years are an essential time for cognitive development and social awareness. Students can use critical thinking to evaluate credible sources, comprehend story motives, and compare/contrast different societal viewpoints.

In high school, a media literacy curriculum can center on communications ethics, especially in shaping public perception and the impact of algorithms on personalized content across mediums. Students can refine those viewpoints by analyzing primary and secondary sources, detecting news reporting bias, and fact-checking and media portrayals.

Despite these potential pathways, most people admit they should have paid more attention to messaging. A Media Literacy Now (2023) survey stated that about 62% of adults mentioned "no opportunity in high school to reflect on how media affects their beliefs, feelings, or actions."

Individuals acknowledge a greater need for media literacy and education research. According to the nonprofit Media Literacy Now (2024), approximately 84% percent of adults believe media literacy education should be in schools.

In addition, this data is crucial to analyze best practices, identify gaps, and provide a roadmap for educators and legislative officials to implement new policies. However, this opportunity opens the door for the corporate sector, specifically communications, to bring in a fresh perspective.

Photo Credit: Getty Image stock irimage. Merod, A. (2023, November 15). California joins a small, growing number of states requiring K-12 Media Literacy. K-12Dive. https://www.k12dive.com/news/california-media-literacy-k12-law/699911/

Integrating the Corporate World with Schools to Enhance Media Communication

Corporate communications organizations can significantly improve the academic system by amplifying and expanding media literacy education. The initiative consists of the following key points:

- Develop grade-level lesson plans and curricula.
- Provide real-world insight into media production and consumption through field trips or school visits.
- Contribute to the distribution of resources.
- Leverage partnerships that integrate knowledge and standards, preparing students for media-saturated environments.

Storytelling is the one powerful concept of media literacy that directly engages open dialogue. You can steer your main message in any direction and control what, how, and why people consume it. Compelling storytelling engages students and enhances their understanding of media concepts. It demonstrates how narratives form and convey critical messages about bias, responsibility, and influence.

One of the things we preach to businesses and clients is the ability to develop awareness. Comprehending the media landscape – traditional, digital, and, most recently, alternative media outlets – allows us to study their strengths and limitations and recommend which outlets would be the best fit(s) to tell their story and maximize audience awareness. Individuals can use the same tactic in media literacy education. Teaching young people strategies for consuming messages empowers them to make informed decisions and avoid unreliable sources.

Integrating Media Communication into Education for a Brighter Future

Implementing media literacy across the board will be challenging, as mentioned earlier. There must be a collective effort between the public and private sectors to prioritize media literacy as a fundamental academic right.

"The more I grasp the pervasive influence of media on our children, the more I worry about the media literacy gap in our nation's educational curriculum," said former FCC Commissioner Michael Copps (2006). "We need a sustained K-12 media literacy program—something to teach kids not only how to use the media but how the media uses them…In a culture where media is pervasive and invasive, kids need to think critically about what they see, hear and read."

Overcoming these challenges requires more than just simple discussions. Whether it is integrating new media literacy lesson plans and curriculum integration across all grade levels, providing new technologies aimed at digital citizenship, implementing new tools to address emerging landscapes, or advocating for legislative support, a comprehensive ecosystem must be built to prepare the next generation to navigate the complex media landscape responsibly.

A Call to Action: Educate, Advocate, and Implement for Change

My call to action is to *educate*, *campaign*, and *implement*. *Educate* yourself through traditional and online methods on media literacy. I intend to work with academic institutions to develop a communications curriculum that centers on media literacy and *campaign*s with government officials to pass essential laws. We must have a society entirely of well-informed, educated critical thinkers.

References

Ellerbee, L. (2009). *Media literacy is not just important. Semantic Scholar.* https://www.semanticscholar.org/paper/%22Media-literacy-is-not-just-important%2C-it%27s-It%27s-to-Ellerbee-Baxter/80dae5671a1612e562e17b65ee9978f136660f22

Bendavides, A. (2023). *Leader's section.* Ed Luminaries. https://edluminaries.drbglobal.net/

Barry, C., Cooper Moore, D., & Khan Seigel, J. (2015). *Implementing Media Literacy in your classroom.* National Association of Media Literacy Education (NAMLE). https://mlw.namle.org/wp-content/uploads/2015/07/implementing-ml.pdf

Copps, M. (2006, June). *Media Literacy: Quotes.* Media Literacy Clearinghouse. https://www.frankwbaker.com/mlc/media-literacy-quotes/

Dictionary.com. (2024). *Media Literacy Definition & meaning.* Dictionary.com. https://www.dictionary.com/browse/media-literacy

Media Literacy Now. (2023, September 15). *Research: National Survey Finds Most US Adults Have Not Had Media Literacy Education in High School.* Media Literacy Now | Advocating for Media Literacy Education. https://medialiteracynow.org/challenge/research/

Media Literacy Now. (2024, September 2018). *What is media literacy?* Media Literacy Now | Advocating for Media Literacy Education. https://medialiteracynow.org/challenge/what-is-media-literacy/

National Association for Media Literacy Education. (2023, August 2). *Media Literacy Basics - U.S. Media Literacy Week.* https://mlw.namle.org/resources/media-literacy-basics/

Get to Know Yesenia

Yesenia Reinoso is an award-winning fourteen-year transformative bilingual storyteller, content creator, practitioner, and entrepreneur. She's currently the founder and principal owner of Y Communicate. Mastering an approximate fifteen-year career in corporate communications, Yesenia worked in industry sectors across the for-profit and nonprofit sectors, including National CineMedia (NCM) and Times Square Alliance.

Contact Yesenia at:

LinkedIn: Yesenia Reinoso or Y Communicate

Instagram: @y.communicate

Linktree: https://linktr.ee/ycommunicate

FROM SURVIVING TO THRIVING: THE POWER OF MOTIVATION IN SCHOOLS

By: Aaron Robbins

The Burnout is Real

Sarah stood at the front of the packed auditorium, facing a sea of frustrated faces. It was her first day as the newly appointed superintendent for the Maple Valley School District, and the district-wide meeting had quickly devolved into a heated venting session. Teachers and staff were airing their grievances loudly: "We're exhausted!", "The burnout is real!", "Why should we care when no one listens to us?" The tension in the room was palpable. Sarah could feel the weight of their words pressing down on her. As she listened to the chorus of complaints about high teacher turnover, endless administrative tasks, and a lack of support, she realized that the district faced highly complex challenges.

Over the next few weeks, Sarah held one-on-one conversations with teachers, administrators, and staff. She heard story after story of staff and teachers feeling undervalued, overtasked, and disconnected from their work and team members. Many felt rigid policies and top-down mandates stifled their expertise and creativity, and the new hybrid work environment added to a sense of isolation and bureaucratic red tape. The challenges were complex, and Sarah understood that a mere change in policy or resources would not suffice. What was needed was a new perspective—a shift in mindset— to create a passionate, engaged, and resilient workforce.

This situation is all too common across industries, not just education. So many of us see work as something we must do, not something we get to do. This mindset is often accepted as an unavoidable reality, encapsulated in the cliché, "A job isn't supposed to be fun...it's called work for a reason." Loving your job does not have to be a pipe dream; it can be a reality. However, to achieve this reality and make work more fulfilling, effective, and collaborative, we must be open to change and learn new ways to understand the concept of motivation—our psychological energy.

Reflecting on decades of research, we now know that the true impact of motivation doesn't come from the quantity but the *quality* of our motivation. Self-determination theory (SDT; Deci & Ryan, 2017) articulates a continuum of motivational regulations associated with three universal psychological needs that, when fulfilled, create high-quality motivation. What Susan Fowler (2014) calls optimal motivation. When our motivation quality is low, our motivation is unhealthy; it is unstable, inconsistent, and requires willpower. When our motivation quality is high, our motivation is healthy; it is consistently high, and we grow vitality and thrive over time.

Understanding the new science of motivation is not just beneficial; it's essential for transforming the workplace. We've developed an initiative that teaches the skill of motivation and has the potential to completely transform organizations into high-performing, high-morale work environments. By helping teachers and staff create work environments that foster high-quality motivation, we can eliminate burnout, reduce turnover, increase engagement, and improve the overall well-being and productivity of staff, teachers, and students. This transformation is not just a possibility. It's a promise.

Empowering Workplaces: Where Motivation and Fulfillment Flourish

As the president and co-founder of Intrinsic First, I lead our consulting efforts in implementing leadership and organizational development initiatives. My role involves guiding organizations to create environments that foster high-quality employee motivation and engagement by developing individuals, leaders, and cultures. Intrinsic First is a boutique consulting firm founded in 2020 by Jimmy Karam and me. With a dedicated team of fourteen employees, we are committed to making the world a better place to work by prioritizing intrinsically motivating environments and fostering cultures where individuals thrive.

I strongly believe in the Ed. Luminaries' mission to revolutionize the educational system because everyone deserves a supportive work environment. This is especially critical in education, where teachers and staff are responsible for the success of future generations. A productive and innovative workplace ensures that educators can provide the best possible learning environment for our children.

The Key Method to Success: Intrinsic First

At Intrinsic First, we transform organizations into optimally motivating work environments through the science of leadership, motivation, and culture. Our process uses assessments, teaching, coaching, and change initiatives rooted in evidence-based practices. We begin with a thorough assessment to support informed, data-driven decisions. Based on this data, we identify targeted classes and workshops that provide a foundational understanding of models, processes, definitions, and skills. Following this, we implement coaching sessions to build and reinforce the associated habits and behaviors. Concurrently, our change initiatives work to create an environment that institutionalizes optimal motivation. Finally, we conduct post-assessments to measure progress and facilitate continuous improvement.

Among our portfolio of culture and leadership assessments, we measure employee motivation utilizing a scientifically valid and reliable survey to assess the fulfillment levels of each employee's three basic psychological needs: autonomy (choice), competence, and relatedness (connection). These needs are proven to be universal across demographics and essential for high-quality motivation (Deci & Ryan, 2017). Just like vitamins and nutrients are essential for optimal physical health, fulfilling these three needs is essential for optimal psychological energy, vitality, and thriving (Fowler, 2014).

Following the assessment, we conduct interactive training sessions for employees, leaders, and teachers. We define the three basic psychological needs (See Figure 1). The need for autonomy involves feeling in control of our behavior and having choices within the boundaries of our values and culture. The need for relatedness involves our connection with people and purpose. When fulfilled in relatedness, we have strong, trusting relationships and feel psychologically safe to take chances and speak openly. Additionally, we feel valued and respected, and that our work and effort have significance beyond ourselves.

Finally, competence is our need to feel that we can effectively apply our skills, experiencing a sense of self, growth, and learning. Competence is not about being an expert; we could be a beginner in a task but still feel highly competent through challenge, learning, and growth.

The Three Core Basic Psychological Needs

Autonomy is the human need to feel in control of your actions and decisions; acting in alignment with personal values, interests, and desires within social contexts and norms. It involves a sense of volition, where you experience your behavior as self-endorsed and freely chosen, rather than dictated by external pressures.

Relatedness is the human need to feel connected to others and experience a sense of belonging, care, and mutual respect in relationships. It encompasses the feeling of contributing to something greater than yourself, finding purpose through meaningful connections, and a shared sense of goals or values.

Competence is the human need to feel effective, capable, and confident applying your skills and abilities in a way that creates a sense of growth and learning. You experience competence when you engage in tasks or activities that are appropriately challenging, leading to development, progress, and a sense of accomplishment.

We also teach that motivation exists on a continuum, encompassing six distinct motivational states that range from low to high quality. These states reflect the underlying reasons or objects of our psychological energy: why we do what we do. Our approach emphasizes that the skill of motivation is not about being motivated—everyone is motivated in some way—but rather about proactively shifting one's motivational state from lower to higher quality through the fulfillment of autonomy, relatedness, and competence. Figure 2 below represents an evolution of Deci and Ryan's (2000) original motivational regulation framework. It builds upon their model by illustrating the relationship between motivation regulations (i.e., states), motivation quality, and psychological need fulfillment.

The Motivation Continuum - The 5 I's of Motivation

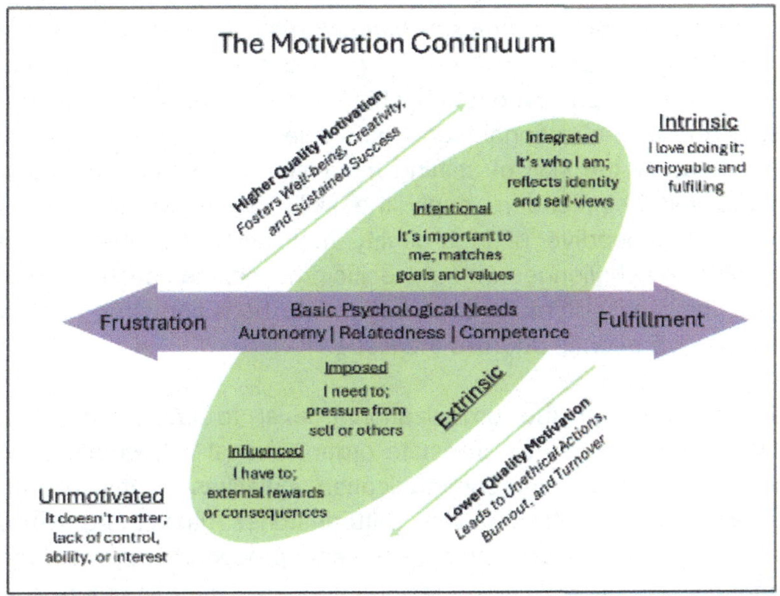

The first motivational state is *unmotivated*: a lack of motivation or intention to act. This lack of motivation may be from overwhelming demands or a lack of perceived value, ability, or control. There are four extrinsic motivational states. The lowest quality extrinsic motivation is *influenced*. Our motivation is *influenced* when the object of our motivation is an external reward or pressure, such as earning a reward, gaining power, or avoiding a negative consequence. The other low-quality motivational state is *imposed*. Internal pressures and obligations such as peer pressure, guilt, shame, or ego enhancement signify *imposed* motivation. For example, you may participate in a work event because you don't want to create a bad appearance or because you feel obligated.

Moving along the continuum to higher-quality motivational states, the first is *intentional*. *Intentional* motivation is signified by alignment with personal values and goals, such as showing up to work on time because you value timeliness and believe it is important for people to be on time for commitments. The highest quality extrinsic motivation is *integrated*; when your actions are fully internalized with your self-concept or identity.

For example, you may mentor a colleague because you see yourself as a leader, and helping others grow is central to who you are. Finally, the last motivational state is *intrinsic*. *Intrinsic* motivation involves inherent enjoyment and interest in an activity (e.g., "I love my job and enjoy what I do"). We provide one-on-one coaching for leaders and teachers to reinforce these motivational concepts. The coaching sessions help individuals apply the skill of shifting motivational states in role-specific situations and help leaders apply the skills necessary to create an environment supportive of high-quality motivation. For instance, if a leader is having challenges with a specific process, the coaching session will help the leader think through actionable behaviors that apply the science of motivation to address the issue.

Finally, we work at the organizational level to implement change initiatives. For example, we translate organizational values into defined behaviors and implement communication initiatives to institutionalize these value-aligned behaviors with cultural stories, rituals, and symbols. We also redefine policies, processes, and procedures to incorporate components supportive of autonomy, relatedness, and competence.

Revolutionizing Systems For Lasting Change and Intrinsic Motivation

Systemic shifts are necessary to create lasting change and foster high-quality motivation in educational systems. Educators and policymakers must prioritize understanding the science of motivation and its profound impact on individual and organizational performance. The traditional approach, which often relies on extrinsic motivators and top-down mandates, is insufficient. Instead, we must cultivate environments supporting the basic psychological needs of autonomy, competence, and relatedness. Educational leaders like Sarah must take deliberate steps to bring about this change. We must move beyond traditional methods and embrace the idea that work can be fulfilling and productive. By focusing on the quality of motivation, we can eliminate burnout, reduce turnover, increase engagement, and optimize overall performance and well-being.

We must create autonomy-supportive environments where teachers and staff can thrive, driven by a sense of choice, connection, and competence. This requires educating and coaching leaders to foster these environments, leveraging specific skills such as active listening, providing objective feedback, and setting performance goals focused on learning and growth. We must rework policies and processes to ensure transparency and open communication. By aligning goals with the intrinsic motivations of employees, we can create cultures that not only support optimal performance but also generate vitality and enthusiasm.

The time for change is now. With proactive efforts to create environments supportive of optimal motivation, situations similar to that of Maple Valley School District can be a thing of the past. This revolution in understanding and applying the science of motivation is essential for transforming our educational systems and ensuring the success of future generations. By taking these steps, Sarah and other leaders can demonstrate that even the most challenged educational systems can be revitalized through a commitment to fostering high-quality motivation.

Free Offer:
As a thank you for exploring the science of motivation with me, I'm excited to offer you a complimentary 'Motivation Matters for You' assessment. This valid and reliable assessment provides a detailed report with insights into the quality of your motivation by measuring the fulfillment of your core psychological needs at work. If you're curious to learn more and apply these insights to your own work and life, please reach out to me at aaron@intrinsicfirst.com, and I'd be happy to share it with you.

References

Deci, E. L., & Ryan, R. M. (2017). Self-Determination Theory: Basic Psychological Needs in Motivation, Development, and Wellness. The Guilford Press.

Fowler, S. (2014). Why Motivating People Doesn't Work... and What Does: The New Science of Leading, Energizing, and Engaging. Berrett-Koehler Publishers.

Ryan, R. M., & Deci, E. L. (2000). Self-determination theory and the facilitation of intrinsic motivation, social development, and well-being. *American Psychologist, 55*(1), 68–78. https://doi.org/10.1037/0003-066X.55.1.68

Get to Know Aaron

Aaron Robbins is an accomplished executive leader with 20 years of progressive experience in engineering, project management, HR, and leadership. He holds an MS in I/O Psychology, an MS and BS in Mechanical Engineering, and is pursuing a PhD in Psychology, Organizational Behavior. He maintains SHRM-SCP, PMI-PMP, PMI-RMP, LSS-BB, and ScrumMaster certifications.

Contact Me: https://blinq.me/VGQG36VwE8p9?bs=db

LOOKING THROUGH A NEW LENS

By: Lisa Polk

Supporting a Broken Early Childhood System: Rethinking Leadership for Sustainable Change

COVID-19 has placed a spotlight on the fragility of early childhood education. Across media outlets, there are stories describing childcare as a broken system. Stories range from the high cost of tuition, the outdated financial model, low teacher qualifications, high staff turnover, and children being injured in early childhood programs. How do we fix such a system? Funding and staffing are critical for quality outcomes for young children. Early Childhood Teachers can have a higher wage but if the work environment and leadership style are toxic, they will not grow.

One of two things typically happens: the educator's work ethic and enthusiasm decline, they leave the field, or a child gets injured or mistreated, resulting in termination. Leading in a broken system using the traditional early childhood hierarchy is not sustainable long-term. In the traditional leadership hierarchy, the director holds all the operational knowledge and decision-making power. All decisions are made by a variety of combinations of top-tier leadership. On the program level, the director has the responsibility. This pressure makes him/her feel as though the person is chained to the program and cannot leave without something falling apart. In turn, this can cause an unhealthy working environment for the director and staff, trickling down to the educational experiences for the children in their care.

Shifting the Accountability Mindset: Empowering Others to Step Into Your Shoes for Systemic Improvement

Early childhood education is my career. I have had the opportunity to work in every aspect of my field. Currently, I operate a non-profit, provide consulting and training, and serve as regional director for a small group of childcare centers near Atlanta, GA. In October 2019, one of my staff was having health issues and accidentally left a child on a 15-passenger van upon transportation from school.

We had a break in our transportation system. The second check of the vehicle did not happen. This prompted an investigation by our licensing organization. Unbeknown to us the Division of Family & Children Services became involved, and we were both placed on Georgia's Child Abuse Registry. I was devastated. Being a leader places you in the position of being accountable for the actions of your staff. Being on the registry caused me to have an unsatisfactory criminal record check, resulting in not being allowed in the center while children were present. Because I was the sole keeper of the operational knowledge, the accountability that a team would hold was missing. This was incredibly traumatic for me and could have led to losing my career. It took four months to get my record restored.

While I was away, the school fell apart. Parents and staff became unhappy and were thinking of disenrolling; the staff wanted to quit. My assistant director told me that she couldn't fill my shoes. That was eye-opening for me. As a leader, I wanted my assistant to carve her own path and not feel that she had to be me. Upon my return, I had a mindset of accountability and strict compliance. I did not want another failed system to occur. The safety of the children is extremely important. The mindset of micromanaging compliance stressed me out and did not garner better results. I knew there had to be a better way.

Solution:

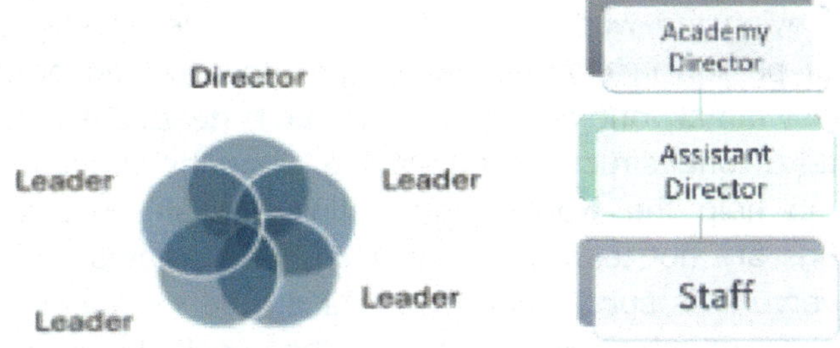

Shared Leadership   **Traditional Hierarchy**

Before joining the childcare programs, I had the opportunity to lead a shared services project that was part of a national network that develops shared services resource hubs in multiple states. This inspired me to create a shared model with a group of diverse staff members and we lead together. Leaders need to secure buy-in across all aspects of the work environment, including team dynamics, parent interactions, family tours and enrollment, operational tasks, and addressing staffing gaps. Lead teachers work in their classrooms for part of the day and handle administrative tasks for the rest of their day. This creates an environment where no one person holds all the operational knowledge.

Currently, we have five leaders including me. At one time we had seven leaders. My new mode of thinking was "If you can't make them accountable, empower them to lead." Since we have been operating in this way, it has been a relief for me. We are working smarter, not harder. A team provides additional checks and balances by a group of individuals instead of one or two leaders alone. Shared leadership is not limited to early childhood but can be applied to other industries as well. When programs implement shared leadership, systems stay intact. As we develop leaders in this way, they are empowered to follow their dreams and do things that they are passionate about. It is an intervention that impacts all aspects of their lives. Morale and productivity increase because they are leading. As the work environment improves, the overall quality of the educational programming increases and enables the staff to be more intentional and impactful as they develop quality experiences for students.

Implementing shared leadership in any context helps to empower staff to lead, improving the work environment and the leadership style of the director or person in charge. Being open to this type of change isn't always easy but anyone can do this! All that is needed is to take stock of your organizational structure and staffing. Bring the strengths of the staff together to help the whole organization flourish. Structure and job descriptions are not teamwork. Empowerment creates an environment where everyone is successful, thus making the experiences within the program more enriching and positive for the people that it serves.

Get to Know Lisa

Lisa Polk began her journey as an early childhood educational coach and consultant 30 years ago as a birth to five teachers. As she found her love for creating high-quality experiences for children and staff, her positions broadened into academy director, regional director, child care program owner, and project leader and director for the Georgia Alliance for Quality Child Care. A common theme across her career has been training and empowering others. Lisa is a state-certified Level 3 trainer, the highest that Georgia awards with special designations to teach curriculum supporting the Child Development Associate Credential, director training, and served as an adjunct professor at a local Technical College. Lisa is passionate about being a voice for being a voice for teachers, children, and families.

This led to serving as the Vice President of Public Policy and Community Awareness for the Georgia Association on Young Children, and held other leadership positions with the Georgia Child Care Association, and sat on the Stakeholder's Board for Zero to Three's Court Teams Project in Douglasville, Georgia.

These experiences led to the development of the non-profit Pollyanna's Place, Inc. where Lisa works with children and families experiencing trauma. She serves as a board member and educational consultant for Rise2Shine, a charity in Atlanta, as they open and operate child care programs in Haiti. Lisa holds a Bachelor's from Mercer University in Human Services, and a Master's Degree in Early Childhood Education from Concordia University. As time permits, she is working on a Doctoral degree in Education focusing on Teacher Leadership.

Begin your journey to a more fulfilling leadership. To find out more information on deconstructing the traditional leadership hierarchy and transforming your team, contact me by using the QR code below for more information on developing shared leadership within your organization.

Contact Me:

MY PATH TO TEACHING: DISCOVERING THE ART AND SCIENCE OF HUMAN LEARNING

By: Dr. Louise Debreczeny

From Horticulture to Special Education

In my late 30s, I realized I needed a career shift from a physical job to something more mental. Managing a nursery where we grew perennials, I interacted with students from special education transition programs, which sparked my interest in how people learn. A particular student, a hardworking 19-year-old who couldn't read, made me ponder the differences in learning and how to help non-readers navigate a text-heavy society. This experience led me to pursue a career in special education.

Education and Beyond: Classroom Learning vs. Real-World Needs

Already holding a bachelor's degree in music, I pursued a master's in teaching, assuming I'd learn about how humans learn. Instead, the program focused mostly on teaching methods rather than the science of learning. When I moved on to a special education endorsement program, I found many strategies for teaching special needs students but still no in-depth understanding of human learning. Realizing that similar strategies were recommended across various disability categories made me question the effectiveness of these intervention strategies. My time as a paraeducator and then as a teacher in special education classrooms highlighted the gap between traditional methods and the needs of diverse learners.

Beyond Behaviorism: Seeking Science-Based Teaching Methods

After earning my teaching certificate, I taught in a special education behavior program, using strategies rooted in behaviorism and operant conditioning. However, these methods felt dehumanizing and only provided short-term gains. My discomfort with these strategies led me to explore other perspectives, eventually bringing me to Daniel Pink's Drive (Pink, 2011). His work on intrinsic and extrinsic motivation made me realize why behaviorist strategies were short-lived. At a seminar on learning strategies for children with autism, I was introduced to Dr. Ellyn Lucas Arwood's Neurosemantic Language Learning Theory (NsLLT). This approach, grounded in neuroscience, language, and cognitive psychology, deeply resonated with me. Over the next several years, I attended Dr. Arwood's workshops and eventually joined her team at her private learning clinic.

My Journey to Neuroeducation: Understanding How People Learn

Working at Dr. Arwood's clinic coincided with the creation of a neuroeducation program at the University of Portland. Encouraged by Dr. Arwood, I enrolled in the program, initially terrified of the dissertation process. The neuroeducation program finally addressed my burning question: "How do humans learn?" Through studies in cognitive psychology, neuroscience, and language, I gained insights into the science behind Dr. Arwood's theories. Despite the emotional and intellectual challenges of doctoral studies, the program confirmed that education must evolve to embrace modern learning science.

Preparing for the Unknown: Equipping Students for Future Careers

As I applied neurobiological learning principles in clinical settings, I witnessed firsthand how these strategies benefited students. With nearly two decades in education, I've become convinced that the lack of focus on how humans learn is a significant barrier to meeting students' needs in an increasingly complex world. The future is unpredictable, and today's students will face challenges we can't yet imagine. Instead of focusing solely on content, we must help learners develop literacy skills that lead to deep thinking and high cognitive function, preparing them to adapt to new jobs and technologies.

Arwood's Theory of Learning: The Neurosemantic Language Learning Theory

Dr. Ellyn Lucas Arwood's Neurosemantic Language Learning Theory (NsLLT) is a groundbreaking framework that integrates principles from neuroscience, cognitive psychology, and language to explain how humans learn. The theory posits that learning occurs through four interactive levels: sensory input, pattern recognition, concept formation, and language. Each level builds on the previous one, creating a comprehensive model of how information is processed in the human brain (Arwood, 2011).

Level One: Sensory Input

At the first level, sensory input, information is gathered through the sensory organs—primarily sight and hearing in a traditional educational setting. However, Arwood's theory acknowledges that learners also process new ideas through movement, such as the movement of hands and mouths, and by observing others' movements. This insight challenges the conventional classroom focus on visual and auditory learning, suggesting that some students may need more kinesthetic input—such as hands-on activities like drawing —to fully engage with new concepts.

Level Two: Pattern Recognition

The second level, pattern recognition, occurs in the brainstem, where sensory data is processed into recognizable patterns. Arwood emphasizes the importance of understanding the visual system in this context, noting that the brain processes visual information through two streams: a fast, black-and-white stream that detects edges and shapes and a slower, color-processing stream that handles finer details (Livingstone & Hubel, 1988). Educators can leverage this knowledge by using simple, high-contrast visuals like stick figures to convey ideas quickly and effectively, especially to younger learners or those who struggle with complex images (Arwood, 2011).

Level Three: Concept Formation

At the third level, concept formation, the brain synthesizes patterns into mental images. This process involves the complex interaction of various cerebral circuits that transmit signals back and forth, forming and refining concepts. Arwood's theory suggests that for many learners, particularly visual learners, this stage is heavily dependent on their ability to create and manipulate mental images. This insight has profound implications for teaching strategies, as it highlights the need for educators to provide opportunities for students to visualize concepts, either through drawing or the use of physical models.

Level Four: Language

The fourth and final level, language, is where mental images are named and integrated into a person's cognitive framework, allowing for communication and higher-order thinking. Language is not just a tool for communication but a fundamental component of thought itself. Arwood's theory underscores the idea that language development is deeply correlated with cognitive development (Clark,1973); as students acquire more complex language skills, their ability to think abstractly and engage in higher-level reasoning also grows. This level of learning is critical because it enables students to articulate their understanding, apply knowledge in new contexts, and engage in critical thinking.

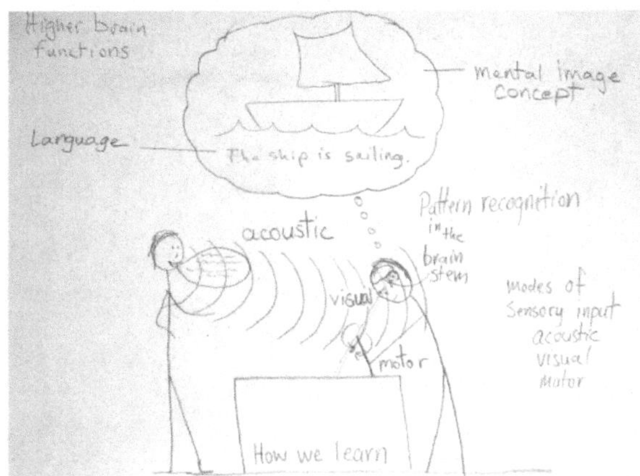

This drawing shows the four levels of learning as described in Arwood's Neurosemantic Language Learning Theory; 1)sensory input, 2) pattern recognition, 3) concept formation, 4)language

Types of Learners

Arwood's NsLLT also differentiates between types of learners, recognizing that not all students process information in the same way. She identifies auditory learners, who represent a small percentage of the population, and visual learners, who can be further divided into visual and visual-motor learners. Auditory learners process sound and visual input simultaneously and often think in words or verbal sequences, making them well-suited to traditional classroom instruction. Visual learners, on the other hand, process information primarily through images, while visual-motor learners combine visual input with physical movement, such as drawing or writing, to solidify their understanding. This distinction is crucial because it highlights the diversity of learning systems in any given classroom. Traditional teaching methods, which often prioritize auditory learning, may not meet the needs of the majority of students, who rely more on visual or visual movement methods to process information. Understanding these differences allows educators to tailor their instruction to better meet the needs of all students, particularly those who may struggle with conventional approaches.

The four types of neurobiological learning systems

Levels of Language and Cognitive Function: A Classroom Perspective

Understanding the connection between language development and cognitive function is essential for creating effective educational experiences. Drawing on the work of Jean Piaget and Ellyn Arwood, we can map out the typical stages of cognitive and language development, helping educators tailor their instruction to meet students where they are.

Early Childhood: Sensory-Motor and Preoperational Stages

In early childhood, typically from birth to around age two, children are in the sensory-motor stage of cognitive development. During this time, they learn about the world primarily through their senses and motor activities

(Piaget, 1970). Language function at this stage is restricted, with children relying on nonverbal communication such as facial expressions, gestures, and vocalizations. Although some children begin to speak during this period, their verbal abilities are limited (Arwood, 2011).

As children enter the preoperational stage, spanning ages three to seven, their cognitive abilities expand, and they begin to develop a sense of agency. They can now perform tasks independently, and their language skills grow rapidly, moving from limited verbal output to a more complex, though still restricted, pre-language function (Arwood, 2011). This is a critical period for language development, as children are building the foundation for later cognitive growth.

Middle Childhood: Concrete Operations and Language Function

Around age eight, children undergo a significant shift in cognitive development, entering the stage of concrete operations (Piaget, 1970). At this point, they develop the ability to think logically about concrete objects and events, and their language function reaches full adult grammar.

This means that children can now use language not only to communicate but also to think and reason. They can understand that other people have different perspectives and needs, allowing for more sophisticated social interactions and problem-solving abilities.

This stage typically lasts until around age twelve, when another developmental leap occurs. During these years, it is crucial for educators to provide concrete learning experiences that align with students' cognitive abilities. Activities that involve hands-on learning, drawing, visual aids, and opportunities for discussion and collaboration can help reinforce these cognitive and language skills.

Adolescence and Beyond: Formal Operations and Linguistic Function

Beginning around age twelve, students enter the stage of formal operations, characterized by the ability to think abstractly and hypothetically. This stage corresponds with the development of linguistic function, where students can engage with complex, abstract concepts such as justice, freedom, and equality. They are now capable of higher-order thinking, including critical analysis, synthesis of information, and the application of knowledge in new contexts.

Interestingly, Arwood's research suggests that not all students reach the formal operations stage at the same age. In a survey of college students, she found that a significant portion remained at the concrete operational stage, while some were still operating at a preoperational level. This variation in cognitive and language function highlights the need for differentiated instruction in classrooms, even at the college level. Educators must recognize that students may be at different stages of cognitive and language development and should adjust their teaching methods accordingly.

Integrating Cognitive and Language Development in the Classroom

The close relationship between cognitive development and language acquisition means that as students' language skills improve, so too does their cognitive function. For example, as students move from concrete to formal operations, their ability to understand and use abstract language grows, which in turn enhances their reasoning and problem-solving abilities.

Educators can support this development by providing activities that challenge students at their current level while also encouraging them to stretch their thinking. This might include using more complex language in discussions, encouraging students to articulate their thought processes, and providing opportunities for abstract reasoning through projects, debates, and other higher-order thinking tasks.

Learning Strategies: Empowering All Learners

Incorporating a variety of learning strategies that cater to different types of learners and levels of cognitive and language function is essential for creating an inclusive and effective classroom environment. Understanding the psychological processes of literacy and the different ways students process information allows educators to design activities that engage all learners.

The Eight Processes of Literacy

Literacy is often thought of in terms of reading and writing, but it involves a broader set of processes that include speaking, listening, drawing, viewing, calculating, thinking, writing, and reading (Cooper 2006; Debreczeny, 2023; Robb 2016). Each of these processes can be divided into expressive and receptive categories. For example, speaking is an expressive process, while listening is receptive. Similarly, drawing is expressive, and viewing is receptive.

Schools typically focus on most of these processes, but one process often overlooked is drawing. Many educators see drawing as merely an art activity rather than a critical component of literacy. However, for visual and visual-motor learners, drawing is a powerful tool for inputting and solidifying their understanding of new concepts. By integrating drawing into literacy activities, educators can help these students bridge the gap between their thoughts and written or spoken language.

The eight psychological processes of literacy

Drawing as a Cognitive Tool

Drawing is not just an artistic endeavor; it is a cognitive tool that can enhance learning for students who process information with visual or visual motor learning systems. Stick figure drawings, in particular, are effective because they are simple, easy to understand, and directly related to the writing process. In some educational settings, such as in New South Wales, Australia, drawing has been incorporated into kindergarten classrooms as an additional symbol set, helping students to develop literacy skills alongside writing (MacKenzie, 2011).

In the Pacific Northwest of the United States, educators trained in neuroeducation have used drawing to help visual and visual-motor learners access new ideas and demonstrate their thinking. For example, a teacher might draw a concept as they explain it and then ask students to draw their interpretation of the concept. This not only helps students process the information but also provides a visual representation that can aid in memory retention and understanding.

Practical Strategies for Integrating Drawing into the Classroom

There are several ways educators can integrate drawing into their teaching to support visual and visual-motor learners:

1. **Visual Dictionaries:** Create visual dictionaries where students can draw and write new vocabulary words or concepts.
2. **Drawing as Pre-Writing:** Encourage students to draw their ideas before writing either instead of or before making an outline.
3. **Drawing for Reading Comprehension:** Students can draw ideas as they read to improve reading comprehension and provide information to teachers about what was understood.
4. **Drawing Science and Math Concepts:** Teachers can draw ideas for students, and students can draw to help themselves understand science and math concepts and solve problems and questions.

Conclusion: Transforming Education Through Understanding Learning

By understanding how the neurobiological learning system works, educators can design activities that align with their students' learning systems. Most students are visual or visual-motor learners who need visual and motor-based strategies to grasp new concepts. Offering activities that engage all the psychological processes of literacy ensures that learners can access concepts in ways that suit their learning systems. Incorporating drawing into literacy programs provides a vital tool for visual and visual-motor learners, empowering them to succeed in an educational system that often overlooks their needs.

References

Arwood, E. (2011). Language Function: An introduction to
      pragmatic assessment and intervention for higher order
      thinking and better literacy. London and Philadelphia:
      Jessica Kingsley Publishers.

Clark, H. (1973). Space, time, semantics, and the child.
      Academic Press, 27-63.

Cooper, J. D. (2006). Literacy: helping children construct meaning
      (6th ed. ed.). Boston: Houghton Mifflin Co.

Debreczeny, L. (2023). Story pictures: A manual for educators, parents,
      and learners.
      Vancouver, WA. INSL LLC.

Livingstone, M., & Hubel, D. (1988). Segregation of form, color,
      movement, and depth: Anatomy, physiology, and perception.
      Science, 240, 740-749.

Mackenzie, N. From drawing to writing: What happens when you shift
      teaching priorities in the first six months of school?
      The Australian Journal of Language and Literacy,
      34(3), 322–340. https://doi.org/10.1007/BF03651866

Pink, D. H. (2011). Drive: The surprising truth about what motivates us.
      Canongate Press.

Robb, B. (2016). A paradigm shift in classroom learning practices to
      propose methods aligned with a neuroeducation conceptual
      framework. (Doctor of Education Dissertation),
      University of Portland, Poerland, OR.

Piaget, J. (1970). Genetic Epistemology (E. Duckworth, Trans.).
      New York: Columbia University Press.

Get to Know Dr. Louise

Dr. Louise Debreczeny, Owner/CEO of the Institute for Neurosemantic and Sociocognitive Learning (INSL LLC), is a pioneering figure in educational innovation. With an Ed.D. in Neuroeducation from the University of Portland, she brings over 15 years of teaching experience, including in public schools and private consultancy. Lou's diverse background—spanning orchestral performance, military service, and a horticulture career—uniquely informs her approach. Her latest work, "Story Pictures," introduces drawing as the 8th literacy, embodying her vision for inclusive, neuroeducation-based learning. Through INSL LLC, she is reshaping education to embrace the varied learning needs of all individuals.

Institute for Neurosemantic and Sociocognitive Learning, LLC
www.institutensl.com
6123 Idaho Street, Vancouver, WA 98661 · 360-910-6752 · Louise Debreczeny, Ed.D. CEO/Owner · louise@institutensl.com

For a free 50 minute consultation with Dr. Debreczeny, please email her at louise@institutensl.com and mention this book chapter.

NAVIGATING CHANGE IN K-12 SCHOOLS: ESSENTIAL LEADERSHIP STRATEGIES FOR POSITIVE CHANGE

By: Dr. Beverly Knox- Pipes

Change is inevitable and necessary for growth and improvement in any organization, including K-12 schools. While implementing change in educational settings can be particularly challenging due to various structural, cultural, and personal factors, it also promises significant growth and improvement.

Leaders must understand these challenges and employ effective strategies to manage change, which can significantly improve the likelihood of successful implementation.

This article delves into why change is difficult in K-12 schools and what leaders need to know to guide change positively, offering a hopeful perspective on the potential for growth and improvement through successful change management. By embracing these challenges, leaders can inspire hope and optimism in their teams, fostering a positive environment for change and highlighting the exciting possibilities that s successful change management can bring.

Challenges in Implementing Change in K-12 Schools

1. Resistance to Change

Resistance to change is one of the most significant barriers to K-12 education. This resistance comes from several groups within the system—teachers, administrators, students, and parents—who often cling to established routines and beliefs.

Fear of the unknown and the disruption of familiar structures drive much of this reluctance. Teachers may worry that changes will add to their workload or infringe on their professional autonomy. They may also be concerned that the proposed changes might shift expectations without adequate support or professional development, particularly those involving technology or new pedagogical strategies.

To effectively manage resistance in K-12 school change efforts, leaders need to focus on several key strategies:

1. **Communication**: Openly share the change vision and benefits, addressing fears and skepticism.
2. **Engagement**: Foster buy-in by involving teachers, staff, and the community in the change process.
3. **Training and Support**: Provide ongoing professional development to equip staff with necessary skills and reduce stress.
4. **Building Trust**: Show empathy and responsiveness, creating a trusting environment where staff feel understood.
5. **Flexibility and Adaptation**: Stay open to adjusting the approach based on feedback to ease the transition.
6. **Shared Leadership**: Encourage collaborative decision-making and shared roles to strengthen commitment and teamwork.

Using these strategies, school leaders can minimize resistance and guide smoother organizational transitions.

2. Ingrained Culture and Tradition

Cultural shift requires changes in mindsets, norms, and attitudes; it is as complex and uncertain as essential. Schools are institutions with deep-rooted traditions and cultures. These traditions can be a source of pride and identity for the school community but can pose significant obstacles to change. For example, a school with a long history of traditional teaching methods may find adopting new pedagogical approaches, such as project-based learning or digital classrooms, challenging. A school's culture influences its members' attitudes and behaviors, making it challenging to shift to new ways of thinking and acting.

Moving a school from a traditional to a progressive culture involves three critical practices for rapid improvement: 1) building a solid community intensely focused on student learning; 2) soliciting and acting upon stakeholder input; and 3) engaging students and families in pursuing education goals.

3. Bureaucratic Constraints

Bureaucratic constraints in K-12 schools can significantly impede change and innovation. Some major barriers include:

- **Top-Down Decision-Making**: Decisions often happen at the administrative or district level, with minimal input from teachers, students, or parents, leading to disconnect and resistance.
- **Rigid Policies:** Strict guidelines on curriculum, evaluation, and standardized testing hinder flexibility and creative teaching.
- **Compliance Pressures:** Accountability measures tied to test scores prioritize meeting benchmarks over personalized or innovative learning.
- **Funding Constraints:** Restrictions on budget use prevent schools from investing in new tools and approaches.
- **Lengthy Approval Processes**: New initiatives require multiple approvals, delaying implementation.
- **Union Limitations**: Contract terms can restrict instructional practice flexibility or adaptation to new demands.
- **Status Quo Bias:** Bureaucratic systems resist altering established policies, limiting opportunities for creative reform.

Overcoming these barriers requires adaptive leadership, collaboration, and policy adjustments that encourage autonomy and innovation.

4. Limited Resources

Implementing change requires significant resources, including time, money, and personnel. Schools in underfunded districts may struggle to allocate resources to support change initiatives. For example, introducing new technology into classrooms requires the purchase of hardware and software and ongoing training and support for teachers and students. School systems know they can't wait; they must use their limited resources strategically and equitably to accelerate student learning. "How much" schools receive is essential; "how well" resources are used is also vital.

5. Professional Development and Training Needs

Effective change often necessitates new skills and knowledge. K-12 teachers face new expectations and more demands from policymakers, parents, students, and schools, including addressing changes in curriculum standards, the emergence of more explicit teaching goals, and shifts in supporting all students in their development. Teachers and staff need professional development to adapt to new curricula, technologies, or teaching strategies. However, professional development requires time and resources that schools may find challenging to provide. Additionally, if the training is not well-designed or aligned with the needs of the staff, it may not result in meaningful changes in practice. Asking teachers to do more without giving them new resources will impact our education system for the worse, and we need to address areas of concern to put us on the right track.

6. Stakeholder Involvement

In education, stakeholders include individuals or groups interested in the success of schools, districts, or the more extensive public education system. This diverse group includes students and families, teachers and administrators and their unions, business leaders, civil rights organizations, and the public. Successful change in schools requires involving the support of various stakeholders and balancing the interests and expectations of these diverse groups, which can be challenging. The world of education looks wildly different today than it did even a few years ago and, therefore, requires strategies that embrace diverse ideas and perspectives.

Strategies for Guiding Change toward Positive Outcomes

1. Build a Shared Vision

Building a shared vision that aligns with the school community's values and goals is one of the most critical steps in guiding change.

Leaders must communicate why the change is necessary and how it will benefit students, teachers, and the broader community. Creating a compelling vision helps generate buy-in and reduces resistance. It is essential to involve stakeholders in the visioning process to ensure that their perspectives and concerns are addressed.

2. Engage Stakeholders Early and Often

Engagement is critical to successful change management. School leaders should involve stakeholders early in the planning process and maintain open lines of communication throughout the implementation. This can be done through regular meetings, surveys, and feedback sessions. Engaging stakeholders helps build trust, address concerns, and generate ideas to improve the change process. It also ensures that those directly affected by the change have a sense of ownership and commitment to its success.

3. Provide Professional Development and Support

Investing in professional development is crucial for equipping teachers and staff with the skills and knowledge they need to implement change effectively. Training should be ongoing and tailored to the specific needs of the staff. Additionally, providing support systems such as coaching, mentoring, and collaborative planning time can reinforce new practices and address challenges. Leaders should ensure that professional development is relevant, practical, and aligned with the goals of the change initiative.

4. Create a Culture of Collaboration and Innovation

A culture that encourages collaboration and innovation is more conducive to change. School leaders can foster such a culture by promoting teamwork, recognizing and celebrating successes, and encouraging experimentation and risk-taking. Creating opportunities for teachers to collaborate, share best practices, and learn from each other can enhance their ability to implement new initiatives. Leaders should also model the behaviors and attitudes they wish to see in their staff, demonstrating openness to new ideas and a willingness to adapt.

5. Utilize Data and Evidence-Based Practices

Data-driven decision-making can enhance the effectiveness of change initiatives. School leaders should use data to identify areas for improvement, set goals, and monitor progress. Evidence-based practices, drawn from research and successful case studies, can provide a solid foundation for change efforts. Regularly reviewing data and making evidence-based adjustments can help ensure the change is on track and the desired outcomes are achieved.

6. Address Resistance and Building Resilience

Understanding the sources of resistance is crucial for addressing it effectively. Leaders should listen to the concerns of those resistant to change and provide clear, evidence-based responses. It may also be necessary to provide additional support and reassurance to those who feel threatened by the change. Building resilience involves helping staff develop the skills and mindset needed to cope with change, including adaptability, problem-solving, and emotional intelligence.

7. Secure and Allocate Resources

Ensuring that adequate resources are available to support change initiatives is vital. This includes financial resources, time, and personnel. Leaders should prioritize resource allocation based on the needs and goals of the change initiative and seek additional funding or support where necessary. Creative solutions, such as partnerships with community organizations or businesses, can also help to address resource constraints.

8. Celebrate Successes and Learn from Failures

Recognizing and celebrating successes, no matter how small, can boost morale and reinforce commitment to change. Leaders should highlight achievements and share positive outcomes with the school community. Conversely, it is also essential to acknowledge and learn from failures. Analyzing what went wrong and why can provide valuable insights and improve future change efforts. A culture that views failures as opportunities for learning and growth is more likely to sustain long-term change.

Conclusion

Change is inherently challenging in K-12 schools due to factors such as resistance, ingrained culture, bureaucratic constraints, limited resources, professional development needs, and the necessity of stakeholder involvement. However, by understanding these challenges and employing effective strategies, school leaders can guide change in a positive direction. Building a shared vision, engaging stakeholders, providing professional development and support, fostering a collaborative and innovative culture, utilizing data and evidence-based practices, addressing resistance, securing resources, and celebrating successes are all critical components of successful change management in education. By embracing these strategies, leaders can create an adaptable, resilient, and committed environment for continuous improvement, ultimately leading to better student educational outcomes.

Lets Chat !!

Contact me: Dr. Beverly Knox-Pipes
drbeverly@bkpsolutions.net.

LinkedIn Profile:
https://www.linkedin.com/in/beverlyknox-pipes/

Get to Know Dr. Beverly

Dr. Beverly Knox-Pipes brings decades of transformative leadership as a prominent voice in a rapidly evolving world. A trusted advisor and advocate, she empowers educational leaders to reimagine teaching and learning, fostering creative, student-centered solutions. Her dynamic leadership as a professor, speaker, author, and former K-12 Teacher and CTO is widely respected across business and education sectors.

Dr. Knox-Pipes shares her expertise through courses, seminars, workshops, coaching, research, and publications. She co-authored the #1 best seller *Ed Matadores: Revolutionizing The Educational System* and articles for *Home Health Care Revolution Quarterly,* which underscore her status as a leader in educational innovation.

Her role as a "leader of leaders" has earned Dr. Knox-Pipes recognition from esteemed organizations such as the National School Boards Association (NSBA), United States Distance Learning Association (USDLA), Education 2.0, *Technology and Learning Magazine*, COSN, Michigan Computer Users in Learning (MACUL), *EdTech Digest*, the Flint Chamber of Commerce, and the Michigan Army National Guard to name a few. Dr. Knox-Pipes' work inspires and drives educational progress, solidifying her place as a visionary in educational transformation.

PREPARING TEACHERS OF THE FUTURE

By: Dr. Donna Vallese

Learning is not a linear process, but the way the majority of K-12 schools are structured is fundamentally forcing students into a box that many of them will never fit. When students cannot fit, educators then start the blame game, saying things such as:

Complex Thinking - Image Generated by ChatGPT 4o

"These students aren't motivated…"

"These students can't learn…"

"These parents don't care…"

"If only these students/parents would just…"

"These kids are different than they used to be…

Through the years, these excuses seem to have increased as our society has exponentially changed, especially in the years since handheld devices and artificial intelligence have become an increasingly integral part of our lives.

If society has changed significantly, which we know it has, naturally how humans learn and engage with it also have changed. While the educational system is in a state of constant improvement and change, it has not changed at nearly the same pace as society, now creating a significant gap.

Consider how we access information now. We grab our phones, open up a browser, type in a few words, and voila! We have instant access to information. However, the majority of our classrooms are still run in a manner where the teacher is the keeper of the knowledge and attempts to pass it on through lecture throughout each class period. Instruction has looked this way for decades, despite research telling us that this is not the way human beings learn best.

Ineffectiveness of Typical Teaching and Learning

Educators can typically describe theories that are critical to teaching children; they can explain constructivism, Bloom's Taxonomy, Piaget's child development, Maslow's Hierarchy, etc. They know the basic facts about multiple learning theories and may even implement them successfully in their classrooms. Educators are also well aware that our workforce needs graduates who can think critically, approach problem solving creatively, collaborate with others, and communicate clearly. So, why does instruction in grades 3-12 still involve mostly lectures when we know that isn't how the majority of the population learns best? Could it be because educators have memorized the facts without deeply understanding how and why they should implement them regularly? Perhaps they have rarely or never seen instruction that truly works? Or, perhaps they simply do not have enough time to prepare for that type of learning facilitation?

Learners need continuous effective instruction that is cognitively engaging, meaningful, and personalized, no matter what age they are.

The educational system must change because our society and learners have already changed drastically. This does not mean that lecture and knowledge-building completely goes away; it means that lecture needs to be broken up into smaller segments and then interwoven with frequent opportunities for learners to

Meaningful, Engaged, and Equitable Learning- Image Generated by ChatGPT 4o

explore, apply, and do something more with new information in order to deepen their understanding and broaden their skill sets. An approach that supports non-linear natural learning will require curriculum topics to be pared down and for schools to ensure teachers have more time to curate powerful facilitation of learning experiences.

Current educators must be supported in how to effectively implement learning theories and for teacher preparation programs must be adapted to continuously model the use of these highly effective practices in their own teaching practices. Student teaching experiences must also become much more robust and meaningful as well to ensure all new teachers have the skills and techniques to be a successful teacher.

Speaking from Experience In Education

My perspective and experiences as an educator are not what most would call mainstream. During my senior year as an undergrad in elementary education, I completed 33 weeks of student teaching (nearly a full year of school) in a competency-based student teaching internship program. I became an educator who focused on project-based learning as I tracked the development of the skills my students were gaining and I spent three years learning how to teach writing effectively.

Once I became a mentor for other teachers, I began to question why they seemed to always second-guess their instructional decisions, yet it was something I started my career confident in. Was it just me, or was it that the program I had attended prepared me extremely well? Fast forward a couple of years, I then studied the competency-based student teaching program I attended for my doctoral dissertation using program evaluation methodology.

As an educational leader, I have had the fortune to work at the school, district, and state levels, leading innovative programs that focused on instructional coaching, personalized instruction, blended learning, wrap-around services, 1-1 devices, performance-based assessment, and standards-based grading. I have been in hundreds of classrooms across grades K-12 in multiple states since 2011 and have identified the patterns in instruction that do not differ drastically from school to school or state to state.

In addition, I have led educator evaluation development and implementation for several years. By tracking scores longitudinally, I found the evaluation areas where teachers continuously score the lowest are on engagement, assessment, and questioning/discussion. It is surprising to see this year after year, in place after place, because these three categories are the areas that can impact learning the most.

As a parent, daughter, sister, and friend, there are far too many people in my life who have been disenfranchised by the educational system. Their disenfranchisement has come because they didn't fit the mold that the system required of them. These people I'm talking about are brilliant in their own ways and either dropped out of school or nearly dropped out because they could not find success in continuously regurgitating disconnected bits of information, did not see the relevance of what they were learning, and were simply bored out of their minds from sitting 6-7 hours per day while their teachers droned on in lecture style.

Sadly, in my son's 14 years of schooling in PK-12, where he encountered dozens of teachers, I can count on one hand the number of highly effective teachers he had. The teachers he did performed best with were those who could:
- explain the relevance of what he was learning
- connect learning to real life
- regularly facilitate student to student discussion
- give students choice in how to demonstrate their learning
- provide helpful feedback with multiple opportunities to be successful
- ask a lot of open-ended questions that generated discourse
- accept all students for who they were in class
- encourage students to express their ideas and opinions
- make grading on each assignment clear in advance
- build strong relationships with students

These descriptors of effective teachers have been well researched (National Research Council, 2000). If it were the case that all teachers embodied these descriptors, my son and the dozens of other people I know would never have fallen or nearly fallen through the cracks. Sadly, I have yet to meet a single person who doesn't know someone who experienced school like my son, my brother, my dad, and countless others.

Changes Needed in Teacher Preparation

One of the many places in the education space that needs some significant change is in teacher preparation programs. Universities who typically only hire researchers to train pre-service teachers must start to bring in practitioners who are experienced in implementing research-based learning theories that effectively facilitate learning; practitioners are the ones who understand the theories, can explain them, and demonstrate them. Teacher preparation programs need to look at some best practices and make significant shifts to include:

- Requiring year-long competency-based internships with opportunities to ensure pre-service teachers can demonstrate effective learning facilitation and assessment strategies
- Incorporating coursework focused on how students learn and how to facilitate that learning
- Ensuring that every graduate completed coursework in how students learn to read and write at all levels and how to provide instruction that closes up significant gaps

Teaching is one of the most complex jobs we have on earth. No two days, classes, or students are alike. Teachers shape and mold learners' brains with every move and decision they make. They have to take into account each child's rate of development, home environment context, cognitive ability, style of learning, pace of learning, and current knowledge and understanding. All of these factors converge in the classroom and can transform day by day. Pre-service teachers must not just memorize the learning theory basics but they need to observe effective learning facilitation, experience these strategies as a learner, and then practice curating the most effective strategies that are engaging, meaningful, and equitable for their students. Learning in K-12 schools is too urgent for new teachers to be figuring out how to teach them in the most effective manner with little support and feedback once they are teaching on their own.

A Year-Long Competency-Based Student Teaching Experience

When someone goes to college to become a teacher, they have to complete student teaching during their final year. Most colleges require only 8-16 weeks of student teaching. But research has continuously shown that a year-long experience is much more effective in producing great teachers (Okrasinski, 2010). Yet, from the moment new teachers walk into the classroom they are expected to perform as well as experienced educators and they are held to the same student outcome expectations as their colleagues who have been teaching for many years. Future teachers must pay tuition for their internship experience while doing the work unpaid. Compare that to professional trades that require a paid 2-5 year apprenticeship program before they get their certification. Or, compare that to doctors who complete a paid 3-7 year residency before they can take the exams for their certification. While most teachers have a mentor for their first year when they start, those mentors are typically teaching in their own classrooms and have very little opportunity to work side by side with the new teacher, unlike doctors, plumbers, electricians, nurses, etc.

With year-long student teaching experiences, pre-service teachers have opportunities to experience working in multiple grade levels. When that year-long student teaching experience is assessed with competency completion in addition to observation, this also ensures graduates have the skills, knowledge, attitudes, and behaviors needed to have a far greater chance of being successful and effective (Okrasinski, 2010). Assessing performance based on outlined competencies helps to ensure that the student teacher can:

- successfully implement multiple teaching strategies
- collect and use classroom and assessment data
- analyze and reflect on data and practice frequently
- provide multiple opportunities for a teacher in training to be successful (Okrasinski)

Programs like this require annual review of the required competencies as requirements in the teaching profession change quickly with new laws, regulations, policies, and administration (Okrasinski, 2010). It also requires solid partnerships between schools and universities who each have a strong investment in supporting the development of strong and effective teachers.

The Call for Revolution

Given the complexity of teaching and the stakes upon entering the first year of teaching, we need to be setting our newest teachers up for success so that we can start to change the fact that nearly half of all teachers leave the profession in the first 5 years. We are approaching a national teacher emergency! Teacher preparation programs are shutting down across the country because they cannot attract enough people who want to become teachers, and schools cannot find enough certified teachers to fill their classrooms.

Facilitating Learning - Image Generated by ChatGPT 4o

Right now, I implore the following:
- Universities, colleges, and teacher preparation programs – require courses in how people learn, create powerful full-year competency-based internships for pre-service teachers.
- Policymakers – hire experts who understand how teaching and learning actually happens to help you adjust laws and regulations to support meaningful, engaging, and equitable educational experiences.
- Current teachers – your professional growth task is to ensure you are an expert in how people learn and that you can facilitate meaningful, engaging, and equitable learning everyday, not just sometimes.
- Current administrators – become expert in identifying and supporting the development of strategies that facilitate rather than dictate learning. Move the red tape out of the way for your teachers and have their backs as they transform their teaching strategies.
- Everyone else – be an advocate for your loved ones' education.

References

Okrasinski, D. (2010). *New teacher's sense of instructional self-efficacy-A case study of competency-based student teaching.* [Doctoral dissertation, Capella University].

National Research Council. (2000). *How people learn: Brain, mind, experience, and school.* Washington, DC: National Academy Press.

Get to Know Dr.Donna

Dr. Donna Vallese is a visionary award-winning educational leader with over 20 years of K-12 experience. As Founder and CEO of Inspiring Leaders LLC, she coaches educational leaders and consults nationwide, driving transformative change in education. A best-selling author and international speaker, Dr. Vallese is known for her work in leadership development and educational reform. She holds a Ph.D. in Curriculum and Instruction, an MS in Technology Integration, and is an ICF-certified coach.

Connect with Dr. Donna:
www.inspiringleadersllc.com
www.linkedin.com/in/donnavallese

REVOLUTIONIZING SCIENCE EDUCATION: A HIGH SCHOOL RESEARCH PROGRAM TRANSFORMS LEARNING

By: Victoria Schulman

Problem-Solution Identification

Science education at the high school level often falls short of engaging students in a meaningful way. Traditional approaches rely heavily on theoretical instruction and simple experiments that do not capture the complexity or excitement of real-world scientific research. Students interested in science are often left conducting basic "backyard" experiments with limited access to advanced tools and resources. This approach not only fails to inspire students but also deprives them of the hands-on experience necessary to fully understand and appreciate the scientific process.

To address this gap, I developed the Advanced Science Program for Independent Research & Engineering (ASPIRE), an innovative research program at King School in Stamford, CT, that is loosely based on the three-year Pavilca model (for 10th-12th grades) for authentic science research at Byram Hills High School in Armonk, NY (Robinson, 2004). However, the original three-year model, which required students to spend the first two years learning foundational concepts before stepping into a laboratory in their 12th-grade year, led to waning interest due to the extended period of theoretical instruction. Recognizing the need for a more dynamic and engaging approach, I transitioned to a two-year program, beginning in 11th grade, where students dive into hands-on, high-level research in professional, university-level laboratories from the start, beginning the summer before their 11th-grade year. This shift was supplemented by an overhaul of the Science Department curricula for core classes that led to early integration of independent scientific investigations in 9th and 10th grades, ensuring that all students, not just those in the official research program, gain opportunities to learn and hone their critical thinking and problem-solving skills. By teaching the basic tenets of research within the core curricula, students are better prepared to learn complex concepts as they encounter them in their lab-based internships once they matriculate into the formal research program.

This revised approach not only maintains student interest but also accelerates their learning by effectively blending theory with practice, creating a more dynamic and equitable educational experience. This reimagined program allows high school students to engage in graduate-level research early on, providing them with access to cutting-edge tools, expert guidance, and real-world research opportunities. By shifting from traditional methods to a more experiential learning model, the program has empowered students to explore their scientific interests deeply and meaningfully.

Introduction & Context

As the Director of Science Research and a member of the Science Faculty at King School, I was tasked with creating a research program from scratch. King School, a private PreK-12 institution in Stamford, CT, serves about 750 students, with a significant portion of the student body in the Upper School (9th-12th grades). Located in a suburb of New York City, the school attracts students whose families often work in NYC, some in high-profile industries such as finance.

My background in Biomedical Sciences, for which I hold a Ph.D., equipped me with the knowledge and experience necessary to design a program that not only introduces students to research but also immerses them in it from the start. The school administration, while supportive, did not have a science background, so they trusted me to build the program independently. With this autonomy, I examined other programs and merged aspects of many to create a unique program that integrates the latest educational approaches, such as the flipped classroom model, and aligns them with the goal of providing students with hands-on, real-world research experiences.

Building the Program:

When I first joined King School, my primary responsibility was teaching core science courses, such as Biology and Chemistry. However, the administration soon recognized the potential for something greater and asked me to develop a research program.

Understanding the importance of teaching students not just what to think but how to think, I began by instituting an in-house Science Fair.

This event was mandatory for all students before graduation, ensuring they not only learned scientific content but also mastered the scientific method. Realizing that the King School Science Fair alone was not enough, I piloted a program that placed students in research internships in New York City, NY.

These internships gave students the chance to work in professional labs, gaining valuable hands-on experience. To complement these internships, I created a course that teaches students the intricacies of research, from data organization to manuscript writing. While this initial program provided essential skills, it became clear that the students' achievements were not being fully recognized.

Pivot to Competitions:

To elevate the program, I introduced participation in external science fairs and research competitions. This shift not only provided unbiased, third-party validation for the students' work but also motivated them to truly excel. The competitive aspect of the program proved to be a turning point. Within two years, students were not only engaging in high-level research but also winning awards at local, state, regional, national, and international competitions, making

King School and the ASPIRE program highly sought-after by underclassmen. The recognition they received also helped them secure spots at top universities and opened doors to further research opportunities.

Flipping the Classroom:

To enhance student engagement and maximize learning outcomes, I adopted a flipped classroom model. Traditional lecture-based teaching often left students struggling to apply theoretical knowledge to practical situations. By flipping the classroom, I shifted content delivery to short video lectures that students watched at home, allowing classroom time to be used for active

problem-solving and application of concepts. This approach, inspired by certain aspects of the Modern Classrooms Project (Farah & Barnett, 2018) approach to teaching, transformed the classroom into a dynamic environment where students could engage with the material at a deeper level.

Challenges and Solutions:

Implementing a program of this scale was not without its challenges. Securing funding was critical, and I successfully obtained the largest donation in the school's history to support the program. Additionally, navigating the logistical complexities of entering students into competitions without an administrative assistant required persistence and creativity. Finally, one of the most challenging aspects was finding high-level research internships for 16-year-olds — a task that required networking and a deep understanding of the scientific community.

Despite these obstacles, the program flourished. The outcomes were remarkable: students have won prestigious awards, published research papers in reputable journals, and even received significant financial offers for their technological innovations. The program not only prepared students for academic and professional success but also instilled in them a passion for science and research.

My Call for Revolution

The success of this program highlights a critical need for systemic change in science education. To replicate this model in other schools, several key elements must be considered:

1)   **Access to Expertise:**
Schools should prioritize hiring faculty members with advanced research experience, preferably at the Ph.D. level. These educators bring not only subject matter expertise but also the knowledge necessary to guide students through the complexities of high-level research. While it is possible for non-Ph.D. holders to coach students to success, having mentors who have navigated the research process themselves can significantly accelerate student achievement.

2)   **Experiential Learning:**
All high schools should provide opportunities for students to engage in high-level, cutting-edge research. This hands-on experience is crucial for teaching students the scientific method and for helping them develop critical thinking and problem-solving skills. Schools must move away from rote learning and simple experiments, which do not fully engage students or prepare them for the challenges of real-world science.

3)   **Equity in Opportunities:**
It is essential to ensure that these research opportunities are available to all students, not just those in private schools or affluent communities. Public schools, especially those in underprivileged areas, should be equipped with the resources and support necessary to provide students with meaningful research experiences. This will help bridge the opportunity gaps between different types of schools and ensure that all students have the chance to discover the joys and challenges of scientific research.

4)   **Integration of Competitions:**
Participation in science fairs and research competitions should be a core component of any research program. These competitions provide external validation for students' work, motivate them to push themselves further and excel, and enhance their college and career prospects. Schools should invest in the resources and support necessary to help students prepare for and succeed in these Competitions.

5)   **Flipped Classroom Model:**
Adopting a flipped classroom model can greatly enhance student engagement and learning outcomes. By shifting content delivery to videos or other at-home materials, classroom time can be used for active problem-solving and hands-on application of concepts. This approach not only maximizes the effectiveness of classroom instruction but also helps students develop the critical thinking and problem-solving skills they will need in their research and future careers.

Conclusion: A Vision for the Future of Science Education

The Science Department and the ASPIRE research program at King School have revolutionized science education by providing students with unparalleled opportunities to engage in real-world research. The success of this program serves as a powerful example of what is possible when education is reimagined to prioritize experiential learning, competition, and hands-on investigations.

However, to truly revolutionize science education on a larger scale, systemic changes must be made. Schools across the country must prioritize the hiring of faculty with research expertise, provide equitable access to research opportunities and competitions, and adopt modern teaching methods to maximize instruction efficacy.

The future of science depends on the next generation of scientists. By giving them the tools, experiences, and opportunities they need to succeed, we can ensure that they are not only prepared for the challenges ahead but are also inspired to push the boundaries of what is possible. The time for change is now, and the impact of these changes will be felt for generations to come.

References

Robinson, G. (2004). Replicating a Successful Authentic Science Research Program: An Interview with Dr. Robert Pavlica. *The Journal of Secondary Gifted Education, XV(4), 148-152.*

Farah, K., & Barnett, R. (2018). *Free blended, self-paced, mastery-based PD, built by teachers.* Modern Classrooms Project. https://www.modernclassrooms.org/

Special Offer:

Until these systemic goals materialize in every school, I have made it a priority to make my services available to any student in the country by helping from afar via Zoom. Interested students can learn more at www.victoriaschulman.com and mention Educational Luminaries when booking an appointment to receive a complimentary consultation and continued assistance at a discounted rate.

Get to Know Victoria

Victoria Shulman, Ph.D., is a former research associate with over 15 years of experience at top institutions, including the NIH, Memorial Sloan-Kettering, and Yale. She has published multiple papers, led U.S. government research, and presented at numerous conferences. Now a high school educator, she empowers young scientists, guiding them to prestigious accolades and inspiring a new generation of innovators through mentorship and research excellence.

Contact Me:
https://linktr.ee/victoria.schulman

SUPERINTENDENTS: LEADING DIVERSITY, EQUITY, AND INCLUSION INITIATIVES

By: Dr. Jerri-Lynn Williams-Harper

The superintendent's role in building strong partnerships with the boards of education is crucial. They lead by example and guide the board in understanding the significance of Diversity. Equity and inclusion initiatives highlight their leadership and influence in this area. Educating the board is one of the superintendent's pivotal roles. School Boards must "understand the implications of DEI issues. The assumption is that minority superintendents have more crucial responsibility because they are "minorities" and have probably dealt with DEI issues personally in their administrative roles. Superintendent of Color providing comprehensive training and resources to help board members understand DEI's historical context and current relevance can be difficult because the experience and lessons cannot be personal but rather factual and data-driven.

By engaging in the swirl of information and misinformation about DEI, we can collectively address the political issues and combat racism and classism in classrooms. Moreover, by acknowledging how education has propelled us forward and celebrating differences that are making us more robust, we can dispel the notion that we are a nation that wants to return to our colonial and racist heritage. This can be difficult for superintendents of color.

DEI initiatives are crucial for fostering an inclusive and equitable educational environment, but they can inadvertently place minority superintendents in challenging positions. These superintendents might face heightened scrutiny and unrealistic expectations to be the sole champions of DEI initiatives, leading to significant pressure and stress. They may be perceived as token hires expected to focus on DEI rather than being recognized for their overall leadership capabilities.

Strong advocacy for DEI can sometimes jeopardize their career, especially if they are seen as too controversial or if influential stakeholders do not receive their initiatives well. The emotional and psychological toll of constantly advocating for DEI in a potentially hostile environment can be significant, affecting their well-being and job satisfaction.

As superintendents, we need to be equipped with strategies such as a road map to navigate plans of action:

Board Members as Advocates for DEI: Provide training and role modeling opportunities on effective communication, conflict resolution, and DEI principles to help board members speak confidently on these issues. Lead by example in board meetings and community interactions, demonstrating respectful and effective advocacy for DEI. Foster an environment where board members feel safe expressing their views and asking questions about DEI topics. Support board members as they engage with the community outside formal meetings to discuss DEI concerns and gather feedback.

Workshops and Seminars: Organize workshops that discuss the historical context of DEI and its effects in schools, addressing topics such as historical inequalities, systemic barriers, and the benefits of an inclusive learning environment. An example of such a workshop could be a session led by a local historian who shares the history of racial segregation in the district and its impact on the current educational landscape. Building coalitions and working with teachers, parents, and community leaders to build a broad support base for DEI initiatives and show that a coalition of stakeholders backs these efforts.

Presentations and Reports: Detailed presentations and reports on current DEI issues within the district help board members grasp the tangible impact of these initiatives on students and staff. Providing board members access to books, articles, research studies, and online courses can further their understanding and commitment to DEI.

Initiating approaches in advocating for DEI: Develop policies actively supporting these goals, such as anti-bullying measures, diversity training for staff, and programs to uplift underrepresented students, demonstrating commitment and dedication to DEI initiatives. Use data to demonstrate the impact of racism and discrimination on student outcomes, highlighting disparities in academic achievement and disciplinary actions to underscore the need for DEI efforts. Present data showing significant achievement gaps between white and minority students, which can help board members understand the urgency and importance of DEI initiatives.

Reviewing Existing Policies: Conduct equity audits to assess current policies and identify areas that may unintentionally perpetuate inequities.

Recommend necessary changes to ensure inclusive and equitable policies, addressing issues such as curriculum inclusivity, hiring practices, and disciplinary procedures.

Superintendents must foster a collaborative environment with the board to develop and refine policies that promote DEI within the district. This process involves the following: The Superintendent and Board of Education must agree on what policy changes are necessary and how to promote the changes within the community. In doing so. there must be assurances that opportunities and resources will be distributed and articulated fairly to the entire educational community. Professional development will be implemented with the acceptance and input of community voices, support staff, and central and all school personnel who will share equally in training and development; so all are aware of new policies and implementation practices. There will be commitments to upholding equitable values and inclusive practices by all stakeholders which will require continual communication and revision as situations change.

Involving students is crucial because they are the key stakeholders who can foster a sense of inspiration and motivation amongst board members with their feedback. Understanding DEI concepts and issues benefits students by exposing them to diverse perspectives and preparing them for a multicultural world. By embracing DEI initiatives, we are not only promoting more inclusive and equitable educational environments but also equipping students with the skills and mindset they need to thrive in a diverse and globalized society.

Monitoring and reporting the progress of DEI initiatives once developed or change is articulated, is essential for accountability and continuous improvement. Superintendents should implement these practices: Collect and analyze data on student achievement, disciplinary actions, and staff diversity. Provide pathways for community feedback and identify trends and areas needing attention. Providing transparent and detailed updates to the board will be essential so discussion on whether implementation is working or revision of policies, training, and practices is necessary. Community engagement is a collaborative effort in DEI initiatives. It is not just about garnering support but also about building a shared understanding and approach to DEI.

Strategies for community engagement include the following:

- **Town Hall Meetings:** Host regular town hall meetings to discuss DEI initiatives, listen to community concerns, and provide updates on progress.
- **Advisory Committees:** Advice and support are essential to an organization. Form DEI advisory committees that include diverse stakeholders such as parents, students, teachers, and community leaders to provide input and support for DEI efforts.
- **Partnerships with Local Organizations:** Collaborate with local organizations to promote dialogue, understanding, and joint initiatives.
- **Addressing Resistance and Claims of Reverse Racism**: Resistance to DEI initiatives, including claims of reverse racism, is a significant challenge that superintendents must address steadfastly, strategically, delicately, and effectively. Strategies to manage resistance include providing context to educate board members and the community that DEI initiatives are not about reverse racism but about addressing historical and systemic inequities that have long marginalized certain groups.

Supporting Board Members in Advocacy defines how Superintendents can empower board members to advocate for DEI initiatives.

- **Training, Role Modeling, and Education:** Provide training on effective communication, conflict resolution, and DEI principles to help board members speak confidently on these issues. Lead by example in board meetings and community interactions, demonstrating respectful and effective advocacy for DEI.
- **Creating a Supportive Environment:** Foster an environment where board members feel safe expressing their views and asking questions about DEI topics.
- **Encouraging Community Engagement:** Support board members in engaging with the community outside formal meetings to discuss DEI concerns and gather feedback.
- Complying with state and federal mandates related to Diversity, Equity, and Inclusion (DEI) is essential for superintendents.

These mandates and dates aim to ensure legal compliance, promote educational equity, and address opposition effectively:

- **Ensure Legal Compliance:** Adhere to laws prohibiting discrimination based on race, ethnicity, gender, disability, and other protected characteristics to ensure legal compliance.
- **Promote Educational Equity:** All students, regardless of their background or circumstances, should have equal access to high-quality education and the support they need to succeed. Effectively communicate the intent and benefits of DEI initiatives to counter misconceptions and build community support. Encourage parents, teachers, administrators, and community members to engage in advocacy efforts, contact legislators, and participate in public hearings.
- **Mitigate Opposition:** Engage in transparent dialogue with stakeholders to address concerns and demonstrate the positive impact of DEI efforts on student outcomes.

Superintendents play crucial roles in advocating against harmful legislation that may undermine DEI efforts by:

- **Establishing Connections:** Build relationships with critical legislators and community leaders, including local church leaders, to provide them with data and information on the benefits of DEI initiatives.
- **Collaborating with Advocacy Groups:** Partner with organizations that support DEI to strengthen advocacy and access additional resources. Use media and public forums to raise awareness about proposed legislation on DEI efforts.
- **Cultivate Supportive Relationships:** Develop relationships with supportive stakeholders within and outside the district.
- **Utilize Professional Networks: Maintain** detailed records of any discrimination or resistance encountered to support advocacy efforts and protect against retaliation. Consult with legal experts to understand rights and options and leverage professional networks for support, resources, and mentorship.
- **Engage in Diplomacy:** Approach DEI discussions sensitively, emphasizing the educational benefits and framing initiatives positively.

- **Educate the Community:** Foster a broader understanding of DEI initiatives through forums, educational materials, and dialogue. Focus on achievable goals and gradually expand efforts to build support and momentum ensuring community involvement in initiatives, and operations.

Loss of talent and diverse perspectives are what we face if we lose sight of inclusivity. Not only are we losing minority superintendents but administrators aspiring to the superintendency. The weight of the situation is severe and controversial. DEI programs attract and retain a diverse body of students and staff. With these initiatives, schools can maintain a diverse and talented population, which can diminish broad perspectives and experiences that enhance learning and innovation. Dismantling DEI programs in schools would exacerbate existing inequalities, reduce cultural competency, lower academic performance, increase discrimination and harassment, and negatively impact school climate and reputation. DEI initiatives are crucial for creating equitable, inclusive, and high-performing educational environments.

"The browning of America has arrived, and the genie will not return to the bottle." Superintendents are vital in leading DEI initiatives within their districts because what we teach children in our homes every day and school should be no different; everyone deserves to shine because of who they are. This is not a time for weak superintendents; we are "statespersons" expected to be well-rounded and well-versed. We foster inclusive equitable educational environments by educating the Board, developing and monitoring policies, engaging the community, and addressing resistance. Superintendents must also navigate complex legislative landscapes and support colleagues of color facing unique challenges.

Standing up to school boards about DEI requires a multifaceted approach that combines knowledge, relationship-building, strategic planning, and resilience. By forging alliances and maintaining a steadfast commitment to DEI values, superintendents can find the courage and capability to advocate effectively for DEI in their school disctrict. Through strategic advocacy and coalition-building, superintendents drive meaningful progress in DEI initiatives, and students thrive in a diverse and inclusive educational setting.

The goal and workings of a superintendent have changed. "You are the change agent." There are two camps, being complacent to "go along and get along" or that of strength, knowledge, and understanding of how to lead communities so teachers can teach and lead educational communities to new heights of understanding that progress means change and acceptance. Where do we learn diversity, equity, and inclusivity on an even playing field if not in school? Schools are purveyors of thought and information. With social media full of misinformation, we should provide all sides of the issue. Class and Race Wars: Are they the final chapter in our educational mission?

References

Gutierrez, C. (2023, December 5). *Best methods of communication when managing projects*. Valens Project Consulting. https://valensprojectconsulting.com/best-methods-of-communication-when-managing-projects/

Sarkar, M. (2024, January 31). *Smart learning in bangladesh archives*.smarttechnology.com.bd. https://smarttechnology.com.bd/tag/smart-learning-in-bangladesh/

Singh, C. (2023, May 27). *Educational equity: Social responsibility and its impact on society*. ReferSMS. https://www.refersms.com/educational-equity-social-responsibility-and-its-impact-on-society/

Get to Know Dr.Jerri-Lynn

Dr. Harper has served as Superintendent of Schools in four school districts, as a curriculum specialist, and as an administrator of Charter and Catholic Schools. Dr. Harper is a change agent. She is the Administrator for "Future Teachers" and adjunct Professor for Great Basin College in the Department of Education in Ely, Nevada. Leadership, management, and accountability during change management are her platforms. She co-authored "Leadership Styles" in 2010 and advocates for Leaders of color in educational administration as the need for more administrators of color is apparent.

Dr. Jerri-Lynn Williams-Harper
Jwilliams434@capellauniversity.edu

THE CHALLENGE OF CHRONIC EXPOSURE TO TRAUMA IN EDUCATION

By: Elizabeth Power

Unpacking Traumatic Experiences

The evidence is clear that "trauma" refers to a broad array of events, far more than abuse, neglect, and child maltreatment.

Since the Adverse Childhood Experiences https://www.cdc.gov/violencepreventio n/aces/about.html) the study connected long-term physical and mental health risks to specific kinds of overwhelming adversities in childhood, the understanding of what might be traumatic has broadened. The ACEs study focused only on the types of adverse experiences shown in the infographic from bettertennessee.com

The experiences the research omitted range from exposure to war, combat, and regional conflict to economic insecurity, medical crises, accidents, natural disasters, and more. Nonetheless, in childhood, they are more likely to influence health in the same way.

Revisiting the definitions used by organizations such as the World Health Organization (WHO) and the American Psychiatric Association (APA) may be more helpful and accurate in defining trauma.

Both groups publish books on diagnoses used in mental health, the ICD-11 (International Classification of Diseases, published by WHO) and the DSM-5TR (Diagnostic and Statistical Manual of Mental Disorders, fifth edition, which is published by the APA).

When you look at what makes an experience traumatic, there are common elements among the definitions.

They all share these common characteristics:

- They are overwhelming, reducing the ability to make sense of the experience, integrate one's emotions, or stay present in the moment.
- They cause people to fear that they might die, be badly injured, or lose their minds.
- Exposure is from seeing, hearing, or experiencing the event.

What determines whether an event is overwhelming and causes someone to fear for their sanity, safety, or life is *subjective*. It depends on the person's age, abilities, support system, culture, and many more factors.

It is the *reaction* instead of the event that makes it traumatic. The event must be so overwhelming that it makes the person experiencing it think they might die, be severely injured, or lose their mind.

Who experiences trauma?

With the added awareness of the breadth of what may be traumatic, the cloud of exposure extends much farther, even into past generations. The impact of one's ancestors' experiences is encoded in the DNA and then passed on to their descendants.

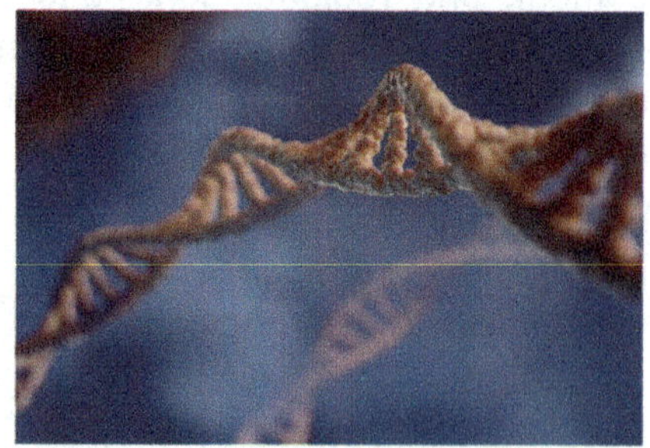

When people talk about "it runs in the family," this may be what they are referencing, this epigenetic impact of the past on the present. In light of this, the real question is, Who hasn't experienced something traumatic? Recognizing universal exposure may be very difficult for some, For others, noting that each person has a unique reaction may risk diluting the seriousness of traumatic events. However, both are factually accurate. They also support broad prevention strategies that support adults and children without requiring a diagnosis.

How does trauma manifest?

There are as many patterns of how trauma manifests as there are people. Age, support, culture, epigenetics, and other factors drive how a person experiences the impact in infinite ways.

The impact of trauma can appear in countless ways, as unique as each individual. Factors such as age, support systems, culture, epigenetics, and more shape how a person experiences and responds to trauma, leading to an infinite variety of patterns.

Developmental stalling.
Neurobiologically, when the brain is in survival mode, learning stalls for everyone. Why? The brain puts all its resources towards survival: no body, no need for a brain! The functions required for learning are impaired until the person can soothe and calm. The Trauma Informed Academy talks about this as Swiss Cheese Development using the metaphor of a stack of Swiss cheese with overlapping holes. Those holes stay until they are healed or made smaller by strengthening protective skills. Development is a life-long process. In a learning environment, this can look like a learner who is immature, or whose abilities are exceptional in one subject and lacking in another, or a learner whose behavior regresses under stress.

Problems with receptive and expressive communication.
One key finding is that traumatic experiences wreak havoc with listening, encoding, and replying. Consider how this impacts learners across the age spectrum. Imagine the impact (different for each person) on their ability to pay attention, respond, create more positive interpersonal relationships, on reading and language arts, interacting with others, obeying authorities, and using intrapersonal communication.

Difficulty making choices.
An essential task in childhood is learning to make choices—to master knowing what we want, perhaps why we want it, and how to make the selection in line with who we are then. Mastering the skills of evaluating the choices available develops critical thinking. Individuals dealing with this often agree to others' wishes, appear unconcerned about what happens, and miss instinctual clues that would normally warn them of risky situations.

Under or over-emotional, lack of ability to regulate.

A common statement in neurobiology is "Whatever fires together, wires together." Sometimes, the brain's alarm system–a very complex set of interactions–gets stuck and becomes hypersensitive, almost looking for things about which to sound the bell and send the body into heightened stress and

anxiety.. This might look like having a "short fuse," which often relates to challenges with self-regulation and emotional literacy. People labeled as "hypervigilant," "touchy," or who refuse to sit with their backs to the door reveal a lot about their past experiences. It can also represent someone who only recognizes "I feel good" or "I feel bad." The specific event isn't the key focus; what matters is understanding that everyone is affected in some way. These feelings act as a "flag," signaling that the person has a history of trauma. This history shows up as behavior indicative of missing skills, or an environment that overwhelms their capacity for response.

Framing flare-ups through this lens makes it easier to recognize the person is trying to *solve* a problem, instead of them *being* a problem. For some reason, their brain sounded the alarm and their body responded to the perceived threat. This is far more helpful than viewing the *person <u>as</u> a problem* because their behavior is aggressive, oppositional, defiant, or cowering.

Difficulty with emotional elasticity.

Overwhelming experiences reduce people's access to their emotions and ability to be flexible about their feelings. They may grow up in an environment with limited knowledge of feelings and their names, where expressing them was dangerous, only in the extremes, or where volatility or the absence of visible emotion was a regular occurrence. Adults can only help children learn what the adults know, so the transmission of skills has a natural limit. Children learn about emotions through their environment—understanding what emotions are, recognizing when they occur, and learning how to manage their intensity.

People of all ages whose "feelings skills" are limited by any of these may show very little emotion, too much emotion, or emotions that seem too strong for the moment.

Skewed frame of reference.

This is a logical consequence of feeling powerless to reduce personal risks in the face of natural disasters, accidents, medical crises, crime victimization, and relational crises. It is a shift in beliefs about oneself. Questions like: "How safe is the world?" "Who can you really trust?" "Can I trust myself?" and "Am I worthy of life?" are the inner concerns children often develop that they carry into adulthood.

Heightened anxiety.

Considering the impact of trauma, anxiety is a natural consequence. Anxiety is an expression of fear. It's about the danger of not knowing—waiting on the results of a test, wondering what's going to happen next, and being concerned about how one might be treated. It is fear of the unknown and a desire for control over one's life. In educational settings, anxiety shows up as inattention, fidgeting, repetitive behavior, restlessness, irritability, and difficulty focusing on instructions.

The Impact of Traumatic Events in Educational Environments

When people are highly stressed, they use what worked before: fight, flight, immobility, or dissociation. Whatever it takes to reduce the overwhelming feelings is the "go-to".

There are four ways that overwhelming experiences impact the educational setting:
1. Behavior management for students and teachers.
2. Less time teaching and learning because of the drama.
3. Lower individual and grade-level academic performance and achievement.
4. Difficulties in relationships and relationship management (students and teachers).

This is the challenge: Everyone is exposed and impacted. The willingness of adults to model effective growth in relational skills has the greatest impact on students.

Five Simple Tools to Address Trauma in Educational Settings

To wrap up and provide actionable steps, implement these tools on a class-wide, school-wide, or even community-wide scale—whether or not part of an organization-wide initiative.

They effectively address the impact of trauma, aligning with trauma-responsive practices to mitigate its effects in educational settings. They benefit students, educators, and all staff when implemented, especially as part of a larger change effort.

- **One**. Greet every person who passes by you—by name (if you know it, learn someone else's)—each morning. Have the class determine four ways they'd like to be greeted, display a poster with the options on it by the door, ask how they would like to be greeted each morning, and respond to the choice each child makes.
- **Two**. Ask yourself how often you wake up with the intention of making someone's life miserable. If the answer is never, why would you assume others do? How does your belief that they do affect the other person in terms of your expectations of them?
- **Three**. Start each class with a centering or focusing short meditation so everyone can settle down—staying regulated is key. Search "co-regulation techniques" and practice them in the class to help everyone focus. 
- **Four**. Take ownership. If you have keys to the building, you're in charge. You set the climate by example for everyone else: Get and stay calm, cool, compassionate, and relational.
- **Five**. Flip the script. When you see someone behaving badly, ask yourself how that behavior might be beneficial.

Does it offer control, power, choice, or some form of safety?

These five tools do much more than they appear to with each supporting one or more of the impacts described earlier. One and three focus on making choices, which reflects empowerment. All five are behaviors that can build trust, show respect, and be collaborative at the same time. One, three, and five focus on self-regulation or emotional elasticity and resilience.

The Trauma Informed Academy's work helps administrators, educators, staff, and students. Our schools see improvement in discipline, relationships, and scores. Educators report less stress and more fun teaching.

Get to Know Elizabeth

Elizabeth Power, M.Ed., is a fourth-generation educator and a Vanderbilt graduate whose work is used on every continent except Antarctica. She supports educators worldwide in trauma-informed practice that reduces the time, costs, and trauma of teaching while increasing student outcomes. Power works online and in-person providing professional development.

Contact Me
Elizabeth Power, M.Ed.
Founder, The Trauma Informed Academy
Fulbright Specialist in Trauma Informed Care
Adjunct Instructor, Psychiatry, Georgetown University Medical Canter
epower@elizabethpower.com / The Trauma Informed Academy
615.714.6389

THE VISION OF AGORA PREP: A VISIONARY EDUCATOR

By: Sylvia Badwi

Redefining Education for a New Generation: The Changing Landscape of Childhood

Children in the 21st century are markedly different from those of previous generations. Their early immersion in technology has significantly shaped their cognitive development, making them more advanced in their thinking and more eager to seek out challenges. This exposure has exacerbated their incessant need for information, fueled by the sheer abundance of data at their fingertips.

The result is a generation accustomed to immediacy and instant gratification. Scrolling through platforms like Instagram, Facebook, TikTok, and Snapchat reveals that today's content is designed for quick consumption. Videos often last only 5 to 10 seconds, catering to short attention spans.

Even adults are increasingly bypassing lengthy posts or videos unless they are particularly engaging. This shift has profoundly affected our children's ability to focus, making them highly distractible.

The Outdated Education System

Despite these changes, schools continue to operate under traditional models that no longer suit the needs of modern students. The rigidity of scheduled activities—where children must arrive, eat, and go outside at predetermined times—leaves no room for choice. This structured approach does not accommodate the dynamic, inquisitive nature of today's youth. Instead, it often punishes them for challenging assumptions, questioning authority, or seeking new ways to solve problems. The current education system is designed to produce conformity, creating followers rather than leaders. Children are molded to perceive reality through the lens of their educators. We trust young children to make significant decisions about their identities but not to choose what and how they want to learn. This contradiction undermines their ability to develop critical thinking and independent thought.

The Need for Change

Every industry—science, technology, arts—has evolved, promoted, researched, funded, and been encouraged by global efforts to innovate. Education, however, has remained largely static. This stagnation is concerning, given that our children, our greatest assets and most important investments, are still subject to an antiquated system of schedules, rules, tests, and dated curricula. Agora also empowers parents who are more educated than ever before and acutely aware of the flaws in the education system. Many of us have experienced the limitations of traditional schooling firsthand. We remember wishing we had more opportunities to explore our talents and passions in school. It is time to trust those instincts and become advocates for our children.

Sylvia knew from a young age that she wanted to be a teacher. Working with children has always been a passion of hers, but her high school experience opened her eyes to the exclusion and marginalization of peers with special needs. Seeing friends with disabilities being bullied or ignored by teachers was heartbreaking. This sense of "self" versus "others" was insidious and damaging. In college and university, she faced racism, sexism, and other forms of discrimination. As an Arab woman, she felt the need to constantly prove herself, often feeling her voice was lost in the academic void. These experiences have fueled her conviction that education must evolve to truly serve all students.

The Innovative Approach of Agora Prep: A Vision for Modern Education

In an era where education systems are often criticized for being outdated and rigid, Agora Prep stands out as a beacon of innovation and inspiration. This leading-edge preparatory environment goes beyond traditional teaching methods, striving to ignite a passion for learning in its students. Serving elementary students from Kindergarten through 8th grade and high school students from grades 9 through 12, Agora Prep adheres to the Ministry Curriculum Guidelines while implementing a unique strategy that fosters interaction and engagement with the content being taught. Agora Prep's distinctive approach is grounded in the "Distributed Collective" mode of learning, a theory developed by Harvard professor Richard Elmore.

This innovative concept is a cornerstone of Harvard University's "Leaders of Learning" course for educators and changemakers, emphasizing the idea that effective learning can occur outside traditional hierarchical structures.

At Agora Prep, the Distributed Collective philosophy is not just a theoretical concept but a living, breathing practice. The school implements this model through various innovative strategies and practices:

1. **Flexible Learning Environments:** Classrooms at Agora Prep are designed to be dynamic and adaptable, allowing for a variety of learning activities and styles. Students might work individually on projects, collaborate in small groups, or engage in whole-class discussions, depending on their needs and interests.

2. **Project-Based Learning:** Projects are a central component of the curriculum, providing students with opportunities to explore topics in-depth and apply their knowledge in practical, real-world contexts. These projects often integrate multiple subject areas, encouraging interdisciplinary thinking and problem-solving.

3. **Student-Centered Assessment:** Assessment at Agora Prep goes beyond traditional tests and exams. Students are encouraged to demonstrate their understanding through presentations, portfolios, and other creative means. This approach not only assesses their knowledge but also their ability to apply what they have learned.

4. **Community Engagement:** Agora Prep values the involvement of the broader community in the educational process. Partnerships with local organizations, businesses, and experts provide students with additional resources and learning opportunities, further enriching their educational experience.

The Impact of Agora Prep's Approach

The impact of Agora Prep's innovative approach to education is profound. Students emerge from the school not only with a solid academic foundation but also with a love for learning and the skills necessary to succeed in a rapidly changing world. They are confident, curious, and capable individuals, ready to make a positive impact on their communities and beyond. Studies have shown that comfort can significantly enhance information retention. At Agora Prep, students are not confined to desks. Instead, they have the freedom to choose their preferred seating arrangements, whether it's relaxing in a rocking chair, using a lap desk, putting their feet up, or even learning in a hammock. This flexible seating arrangement ensures that students are happier, more comfortable, and, therefore, more receptive to absorbing knowledge.

Developing 21st Century Skills

Preparing students for the future means equipping them with essential 21st-century skills: Critical Thinking, Collaboration, Creativity, and Communication. These skills are at the forefront of our educational philosophy.

- **Critical Thinking:** Regular debates, book reviews, and discussions on current affairs are some of the ways we foster critical thinking.
- **Collaboration:** We emphasize teamwork and collective problem-solving, ensuring that students understand the value of collaboration.
- **Creativity:** provides numerous opportunities for students to express themselves and think outside the box, whether through art, music, writing, or innovative projects.
- **Communication:** Effective communication is a vital skill for future entrepreneurs and leaders. We focus on developing students' ability to articulate their ideas clearly and confidently, preparing them for various roles in society.

Leveraging Technology, Gardening, Cooking and Financial Literacy

In the modern educational landscape, technology plays a pivotal role. At Agora Prep, we ensure that technology is accessible and available to all students, leveraging its power to enhance learning and knowledge acquisition.

One of the standout features of our curriculum is the inclusion of gardening and cooking. Students engage in gardening, learning about aquaponics and hydroponics, and developing an appreciation for environmental sustainability. In the kitchen, they cultivate culinary skills, from basic cooking techniques to baking, gaining practical life skills that are essential for their future.

Financial literacy is another critical area often neglected in traditional education. At Agora Prep, we teach students about investments, savings, and earnings, equipping them with essential life skills. Understanding how to manage money is vital for success in adulthood, and our practical approach ensures that students are well-prepared to handle their financial futures.

Mindfulness and Meditation: Mental Health Focus

Mental health is a cornerstone of our educational philosophy. We coach students in mindfulness, stretching, and emotional self-regulation techniques, helping them develop strategies to support their mental well-being. These practices are integrated into their daily learning, promoting overall health and emotional stability. At Agora Prep, we celebrate all learning differences and disabilities. Our inclusive environment recognizes that children develop at their own pace, and we provide the support and encouragement they need to thrive. Learning happens through interaction and collaboration, not just from behind a desk. We welcome children of all needs and skills, encouraging them to share their talents with their peers and coaches, and fostering a community where every ability is seen as awesome.

A Model for the Future

As educational systems around the world grapple with the challenges of the 21st century, Agora Prep offers a compelling model for the future. By prioritizing curiosity, community, and cooperation, Agora Prep is transforming the way we think about education. It is a place where students are not just taught but inspired to learn, setting the stage for a lifetime of discovery and growth.

Agora Prep is more than just a school; it is a visionary institution that exemplifies the best of modern educational practices. Through its commitment to innovative teaching methods and its dedication to nurturing the innate curiosity of children, Agora Prep is preparing the leaders and changemakers of tomorrow.

It is time to acknowledge what we've known for decades: schools need to pivot and evolve to meet the needs of our new generation of thinkers, leaders, and inventors. We need more experiential learning and life-skill development and fewer archaic philosophies. The education system must support and integrate students of all abilities, celebrating their strengths and helping them explore their purpose. **Enough schooling, more learning.** This must be the way forward. Only by embracing these changes can we prepare our children for a future where they can thrive, innovate, and lead. The time for transformation in education is now!

Get to Know Sylvia

Sylvia Badwi, founder of Agora Prep, is a trailblazer in the field of education. Her journey began in 2001 with her Bachelor of Education thesis called "Engagement in Learning".

Sylvia's passion was reignited when she graduated from Harvard University with a post-degree program in 2020. Armed with new insights and a renewed sense of purpose, Sylvia set out to create a pedagogy that caters to the needs of every child. As an Arab Canadian woman, she faced numerous challenges throughout her life. Her late diagnosis of ADHD as an adult developed a deep empathy for differentiated learners. Through her foundation and educational initiatives, Sylvia is paving the way for a more inclusive and effective approach to education, where every child's potential is recognized and nurtured.

Connect with me to revolutionize education today:

THERE IS A POWER IN KINDNESS, BUT EVEN STRONGER POWER WHEN WE ARE UNITED

By: Nebiyou Timotewos

Transforming Adversity into Empowerment: A Journey Towards Building a Social Purpose-Driven Society

In this capitalist society, we often feel forced to choose between helping others and growing individually, as if kindness and wealth can't coexist, as if kindness is a weakness. This mindset has kept us trapped in a race, always chasing the next big thing. When did we, as a society, start avoiding kindness with excuses like "I need to help myself first," or "I have my own problems too"? I don't understand, nor do I want to. Have we forgotten that when we help others, we're really helping ourselves? We've become trapped in a never-ending cycle focused on personal gains and a "me me me" mentality, often forgetting the power of unity and the collective good. Instead of asking, "How can I help others when I have my own work?" we should be thinking, "How can I weave kindness into my daily life and interactions?" Being kind to others doesn't mean dropping everything, it means finding ways to integrate kindness into our routines and conversations. We need to shift toward a socially purpose-driven model, where personal and community success are deeply intertwined. The day we recognize the true power of kindness and understand that it's our collective strength is the day everything changes.

In this chapter, I will share my personal story and discuss the organizations and initiatives I founded around the theme of kindness. I will also outline my vision for a world driven by social purpose and explain why it's essential for us to act together today to create a better and friendlier tomorrow.

From Adversity to Action: Building a Social Purpose-Driven Society Through Youth Empowerment and Resilience

My name is Nebiyou Timotewos, a 19-year-old, multiple international award-winning humanitarian, a national hero, a youth role model of the year, 5 Times Leadership Award winner, and the first-ever youth community all-star in Canada before becoming Canadian, among other accolades. However, my life hasn't always been easy.

I was born in Ethiopia, Hawassa, on October 18, 2004, alongside my six siblings originally, but two unfortunately passed away at a very young age, leaving me with four siblings. My dad was originally a mayor of a city in the southern nation but resigned due to the team being corrupted, and he didn't want to take any part in it because he always believed in doing good. This forced my parents to open a restaurant cafe to make a living until my dad got the opportunity to work as a diplomat at the Ministry of Foreign Affairs. However, it was in Addis Ababa, a different city, so he had to move alone, leaving us with only our mom for a while. Those were long 3 and a half years, but time eventually passed and the clouds cleared as my dad became a diplomatic accountant and started getting placed at different locations.

We were placed in Yemen, and our whole family moved there. It was a good time until we were shortly met by the unfortunate war. When the war broke out, every embassy closed, and everyone left. But my dad, as the embassy leader, had a choice to make. The Ethiopian government sent jets for us to close the embassy and leave, but my dad refused because he knew that if he closed the Ethiopian embassy, there would be no way out for all these innocent people. My dad made the brave choice to keep the embassy open, allowing more than 6000 people to evacuate with their families safely.

Eventually, once everyone who wanted to leave had left, we closed the embassy and also left. Those few months were hectic as our car, our house, and my school were bombed. I witnessed the horrifying, graphic deaths of my close family and friends right before my eyes. But with the grace of God, we were fortunate enough to survive. After we left Yemen, we stayed in Ethiopia for a few months, during which my dad won the National Hero Award in 2015.

After that, we moved to Ireland where my dad was sick, near death, and faced other challenges. When we eventually moved to Canada, we were placed in a shelter for 7 months until we eventually found a place to stay.

My mom baked bread to sell, and my dad worked night jobs to maintain our family's livelihood. They sacrificed their lives so we could have a better future, and we survived on community donations. In 2020, I lost both my grandparents on the same day, followed by another loss on my mom's side just a month later. This was incredibly difficult. Not being able to attend their funerals back home because we weren't citizens at the time made it even harder. This turmoil was a challenging experience that deeply affected me.

I still didn't let the trauma or hardship define who I was but rather used it as motivation to excel and help the community that once assisted us. I graduated high school with honours and got into university. I began helping my community as young as the age of 15 when I volunteered to help homeless people by providing food, clothing, etc. Once I entered university, I expanded my community involvement. I volunteered with the PSAC, became a youth ambassador with peacebuilders, a project advisory council member with Black Legal Action, the director of the largest faculty at York University, a campus commissioner at York University, vice president of my program at York University, and an event director at the Ethiopian Association at York, among other roles. In the summer of 2023, I still felt like I wasn't doing enough for my community.

In November 2023, I took things to the next level by founding Brothers4Brothers, an organization focused on youth mental health and breaking the stigma surrounding it. Communities Care was launched in February 2024 to reach vulnerable youth in immediate need through kindness Kits. These Kits include essential items such as hygiene products and school supplies, as well as access to mentorship programs. Brothers4Brothers and Communities Care were established to create a society driven by social purpose, empowering youth to cultivate kindness, resilience, and active community engagement. I believe that giving young people hope and equipping them with the skills they need will help them become the leaders of not just tomorrow, but today.

Key milestones include the development of multiple cohorts of mentorship programs through Brothers4Brothers, the expansion of Communities Care into Africa, and partnerships with local organizations. Both organizations have helped thousands of youth worldwide, creating a ripple effect of

kindness. I started these organizations because I understand firsthand the power of community support and the importance of providing spaces where young people can feel seen and heard. Having faced a traumatic childhood without the resources or anyone to turn to, I wanted to pay it forward and be the person I wish I had for the youth of today.

Revolutionizing Education for Holistic Growth: The Vital Role of Social Purpose in Shaping Compassionate and Responsible Leaders

As the Leadership Education Equity Ambassador at York University, I recognize the vital role of social purpose in revolutionizing education. It is essential to create environments that prioritize not just academic success but also the holistic development of students. By integrating social purpose into education, we foster emotional, social, and ethical growth, preparing young people to lead with compassion and a sense of responsibility.

Programs like Communities Care and Brothers4Brothers illustrate the transformative power of education rooted in social purpose. These initiatives specifically target marginalized youth populations in Canada, emphasizing the importance of community engagement and support.

School boards and teachers are crucial in this integration. By adopting curricula that address social issues and promoting awareness of community challenges, educators can inspire students to become active participants in their communities.

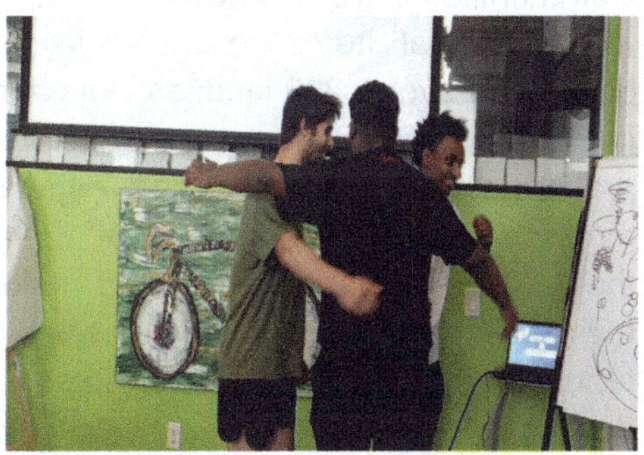

Moreover, fostering a culture of kindness within schools is fundamental. When educators model and encourage acts of kindness, they create an inclusive atmosphere where students feel valued and supported. This positive environment significantly contributes to improved mental health and a strong sense of belonging among students. Initiatives that promote kindness and empathy not only enhance individual well-being but also cultivate a community spirit that empowers students to take responsibility for one another.

Our programs have already impacted dozens of young people, many of whom share transformative stories about how these initiatives have positively influenced their lives. As we continue to expand our reach, our goal is to connect with even more youth and create lasting, positive change in the community. By nurturing socially conscious leaders who embody kindness and a commitment to social purpose, we can build a more compassionate and responsible society for the future.

Overcoming Obstacles and Achieving Impact: The Journey of Implementing Brothers4Brothers and Communities Care Initiatives

Brothers4Brothers, launched in November 2023, and Communities Care, which began six months ago, have profoundly impacted the lives of countless youth. Brothers4Brothers has run three cohorts, offering mentorship and community engagement for young men across the city. Through these cohorts, young men who once felt isolated and hopeless are now motivated to step up as leaders and make a difference in their communities.

Communities Care extends this mission by providing kindness kits filled with essential items to those in need. Since its inception, we've distributed over 1,200 kindness kits across Canada and 300 kits to youth in Africa, bringing hope and relief to vulnerable youth globally. Both programs are close to my heart, especially as they stem from a promise I made to myself in 2017 when, at 12 years old, I left the shelter. I vowed that one day I would return and make a difference for youth who, like myself, felt unseen and unsupported. Today, I work tirelessly with my team to create lasting change, determined not to let that young dreamer down.

These social purpose-driven initiatives have sparked a transformation in many participants' lives. Youth who previously struggled with depression or suicidal thoughts now express new hope and purpose. Some have even shared how Brothers4Brothers has enabled them to stop taking antidepressants, crediting the community support and mentorship for their positive outlook. The results have been both measurable and deeply moving.

Beyond individual transformations, we see a growing ripple effect, as graduates often return as mentors, committed to supporting others. The youth-centric, fully youth-led nature of both organizations has cultivated a unique bond, allowing participants to feel understood, empowered, and supported by peers who share their experiences.

A Call for Collective Action: Building a Movement for a Social Purpose-Driven Society Through Education and Community

We need stronger financial backing for programs that build a society rooted in social purpose, as well as policy changes that bring these values into school curricula. Society also needs to move toward a wider acceptance of open discussions about mental health and community responsibility, beginning with greater representation in education, media, and public conversation.

I urge communities, educators, and policymakers to prioritize creating a society driven by social purpose. Supporting initiatives like Communities Care and Brothers4Brothers allows us to empower the next generation to lead with kindness, resilience, and a strong sense of responsibility. While no one person can change the world alone, together, we can build a movement that transforms lives and strengthens communities with compassion. When we embrace the power of kindness, everyone benefits. By helping others, we create a cycle of positive change that uplifts us all. Imagine a world where social purpose drives everything we do, a world where kindness, compassion, and meaningful connections are at the core of our actions. This is what truly matters. Material things, achievements, and titles will all fade away in time, but what will be remembered is how we made people feel, the impact we left, and the lives we touched.

Our legacy will not be built on what we had or accomplished alone but on the kindness we shared and the difference we made.

My challenge for you is this:

As you finish reading this chapter, put the book down for a moment and do something for someone else. Take a small step, buy a coffee and muffin for someone in need, call a loved one to check in, or offer a heartfelt compliment to a friend. These small acts of kindness create ripples that can change the world, starting with the person right next to you.

Offer

After completing the kindness challenge, share it using #ThereIsAPowerInKindness and tag me! I'll personally reach out to set up a one-on-one call to explore how we can grow this movement in your area and support you in making your community a better place.

Get to Know Nebiyou

Nebiyou Timotewos, 19, is an international award-winning humanitarian and founder of Brothers4Brothers and Communities Care, organizations that empower vulnerable youth through immediate support and mentorship. His journey from war in Yemen to a Canadian shelter fuels his commitment to uplift others. He aims to spread kindness globally and envisions a future in politics that aligns society with a social purpose-driven model, guided by his slogan,
"There Is A Power In Kindness."

<u>Contact Me</u>
Website: Nebiyoutimotewos.com
Instagram: Nebiyoutimotewos
Linkedin: NebiyouTimotewos
<u>www.Brothers4Brothers.org</u>
<u>www.Communitiescare.org</u>

112

UNLOCKING COGNITIVE POTENTIAL: RETHINKING EDUCATION THROUGH WORKING MEMORY AND METACOGNITIVE STRATEGIES

By: María Angélica Benavides, Ed.D
known as Dr. B.

The Foundation of My Research: A Journey into Understanding Working Memory and Metacognition

In the course of my academic and professional journey, I recognized a significant gap in educational practices: the often-overlooked impact of working memory (WM) on student learning. This realization became the foundation for my dissertation, which I completed in 2013, focusing on educators' understanding of poor WM and the effectiveness of metacognitive interventions. My intense research journey led me to explore the critical role that WM plays in academic success, as well as the essential need for metacognitive strategies to support struggling learners.

My research was rooted in a qualitative, phenomenological study designed to investigate how educators understand and apply interventions for students with WM deficits. Through interviews and focus groups with public and charter school teachers, I explored the practical challenges teachers face when working with students who struggle to retain and process information.

The study revealed an urgent need for cognitive-based strategies in classrooms, as over 90% of the educators I interviewed expressed a lack of preparation and support in addressing WM-related issues. They felt overwhelmed, with limited time to address the specific needs of students struggling with WM, largely due to accountability pressures and other educational mandates.

The findings of my dissertation highlighted a crucial insight: educators often lacked awareness of how WM deficits manifest and how they could support students using specific metacognitive strategies. Instead, struggling students were frequently labeled with broader learning disabilities without investigating the root cause of their challenges. This tendency toward premature labeling often overlooked targeted interventions that could address the WM challenges directly, thereby supporting students' needs more effectively. My dissertation from 2013 underscored the importance of equipping educators with knowledge of WM and metacognitive strategies. I advocated for professional development that would train teachers to recognize and address WM issues through specific, evidence-based interventions. This approach, I argued, would enable educators to design instructional strategies that support cognitive development and foster student success, rather than defaulting to labels that might not address the underlying cognitive challenges.

This foundational research has remained a guiding principle in my work, inspiring me to pursue further opportunities to share these insights and help reshape the educational system to better accommodate the diverse cognitive needs of all learners.

The Need for a New Educational Paradigm

Education, as it stands today, often falls short of meeting the diverse cognitive needs of all students. Many learners struggle due to challenges with working memory (WM), a cognitive function essential for retaining and processing information in real-time. Deficits in WM can affect a student's ability to complete complex tasks, follow instructions, and stay engaged in learning. However, schools rarely prioritize WM-based interventions or provide educators with strategies that explicitly support these cognitive needs.

In reimagining an educational system that truly serves all students, it's essential to adopt a cognitive-focused approach that incorporates behavioral, cognitive, and constructivist theories in practical and accessible ways. By bringing these theories to life through classroom strategies and institutional support, educators can  not only support WM but also foster a learning environment that enhances student achievement and engagement.

This chapter explores how leadership, classroom strategies, and theoretical frameworks can collectively create a revolutionary educational paradigm.

The Role of Leadership in Cognitive-Based Educational Reform

Strong, visionary leadership is crucial in reshaping education to support WM and metacognition. Leaders can play a pivotal role by championing the importance of cognitive science in education, creating policies that encourage innovative teaching practices, and providing the resources necessary for implementing WM-based interventions.

1. **Establishing a Culture of Cognitive Awareness**: Leaders can foster a school culture that prioritizes understanding cognitive processes like WM. Through workshops, seminars, and professional development, leaders can ensure that educators feel knowledgeable and empowered to address these issues in the classroom.
2. **Empowering Educators**: Leadership must emphasize the importance of WM by providing educators with resources and time to implement WM-friendly instructional strategies. By investing in tools and materials, leaders can facilitate the adoption of cognitive support strategies, from visual aids and manipulatives to digital tools that allow students to process information incrementally.
3. **Advocating for Continual Learning and Professional Development**: Leaders who promote ongoing professional development in WM and cognitive strategies contribute to a progressive learning environment where teachers continuously update and refine their skills. This can include learning about new research, experimenting with cognitive-based teaching techniques, and collaborating with other educators to share insights.

When leaders champion cognitive awareness, they create an environment where educators feel supported and motivated to explore strategies that cater to WM and overall cognitive development. This shift benefits students and empowers teachers to become agents of change within their own classrooms.

Avoiding Premature Labeling: Identifying Challenges Before Diagnosing Disabilities

One of the major issues facing today's educational system is the tendency to diagnose students with specific learning disabilities without fully understanding the root causes of their academic challenges. While learning disabilities are certainly real and impactful for many students, there are instances where cognitive

challenges—such as those related to WM—may be misunderstood or misclassified.

Rather than rushing to label students, educators can adopt a more investigative approach. Many students struggle because of temporary or situational issues with WM, attention, or processing speed rather than underlying disabilities. When educators are trained to recognize and address these specific cognitive needs, they can provide targeted interventions that may resolve the issue without requiring a formal diagnosis.

1. **Fostering an Investigative Approach**: Teachers should be encouraged to ask *why* a student is struggling rather than jumping to conclusions. Observing students' interactions with tasks and pinpointing where breakdowns occur in WM or focus can help educators implement specific strategies tailored to the student's needs.

2. **Providing WM-Based Support Before Diagnosis**: Schools can implement WM-friendly strategies, such as breaking tasks into smaller steps, using repetition, and allowing for frequent reviews, to support students without assuming a disability. This cognitive-first approach allows for proactive, supportive interventions that may prevent students from needing specialized diagnoses.

3. **Building Awareness of Cognitive Diversity**: Educators can be empowered to see student struggles not as fixed limitations but as areas where cognitive-based teaching strategies can make a

difference. By recognizing and addressing the underlying cognitive needs of students, schools can help reduce the incidence of misdiagnosis and better support student success across the board.

Taking the time to assess cognitive needs before labeling allows educators to provide appropriate interventions tailored to specific challenges. This approach not only addresses students' immediate needs but also upholds a more inclusive, supportive educational environment.

Integrating Behavioral, Cognitive, and Constructivist Theories for Practical Teaching

Educational theories provide invaluable insights into how students learn and retain information. By integrating behavioral theory, cognitive theory, and constructivism in a cohesive, practical framework, teachers can create instructional designs that directly support WM and facilitate metacognitive growth. Here's how each theory contributes to the revolutionary educational approach:

1. **Behavioral Theory**: Behavioral principles, such as reinforcement, are effective for establishing routines and supporting memory retention in students. By reinforcing positive behaviors—like organization, task completion, and focus—teachers can help students develop habits that enhance WM. For example, using reward systems for remembering multi-step instructions can help students practice and internalize memory skills.

2. **Cognitive Theory**: Cognitive theory emphasizes the importance of understanding the mind's internal processes. Educators can use this theory to structure information in ways that reduce cognitive overload, a frequent challenge for students with poor WM. Techniques like chunking (breaking information into smaller, manageable pieces), using mnemonics, and frequent repetition help reinforce key concepts and support long-term retention.

3. **Constructivism**: Constructivist approaches, which encourage active learning and knowledge-building through experience, are

instrumental for fostering metacognitive skills. Teachers can use constructivist principles to create interactive lessons that allow students to connect new information with prior knowledge. For example, group activities, discussions, and problem-solving exercises not only support WM but also encourage students to think critically about their learning processes.

By blending these theories into a cohesive, student-centered approach, educators can design lessons that are both supportive of WM needs and conducive to deeper learning.

Supporting Working Memory Through Classroom and Institutional Strategies

Supporting WM in the classroom requires both specific teaching methods and broader institutional strategies. Here are practical ways to apply cognitive-based interventions at both levels:

1. **Classroom Techniques to Support Working Memory**:
   - **Chunking Information**: Teachers can break down complex concepts into smaller, digestible units that are easier for students to retain. For instance, in a math class, rather than introducing an entire formula at once, educators can teach each component in steps.
   - **Frequent Review and Repetition**: Repeating key concepts in varied formats helps reinforce learning. Teachers might review core ideas at the start and end of each lesson or use spaced repetition strategies.
   - **Visual Aids and Graphic Organizers**: Visuals support WM by helping students organize and recall information. Tools like flowcharts, diagrams, and graphic organizers provide a clear structure, aiding students who struggle with processing sequential or complex information.

2. **Institutional Strategies to Support Cognitive Development**:
   - **Professional Development Programs**: Schools can offer professional development focused on cognitive science, equipping educators with WM strategies to

improve instructional effectiveness.

- **Collaboration Opportunities**: Educators benefit from sharing strategies and discussing their experiences with WM interventions. Schools can facilitate collaboration through workshops or regular meetings.
- **Dedicated Cognitive Support Resources**: Schools can provide tools such as WM-focused learning materials, apps, and instructional guides that support cognitive development. Additionally, offering "cognitive kits" with manipulatives and visual aids can enhance classroom activities.

These strategies create a cohesive system of support where WM challenges are addressed consistently, providing struggling students with the scaffolded learning they need to succeed.

Conclusion: Revolutionizing Education for Cognitive Equity

By understanding and integrating WM and metacognitive principles into everyday teaching, educators can provide more equitable support for struggling learners. This chapter has outlined the critical role of leadership in fostering a culture of cognitive awareness, demonstrated practical ways to apply educational theories in classrooms, and highlighted actionable strategies for supporting WM at both individual and institutional levels.

Revolutionizing education to support WM and cognitive diversity is not only a transformative approach but a necessary one. When educators are empowered with cognitive insights and practical interventions, and when leaders champion a cognitive-first mindset, the educational system becomes a more inclusive space where every student can thrive. Through collective action, we can reshape education to better support and celebrate cognitive differences, paving the way for future-ready learning environments.

Call to Action

Are you passionate about sharing your expertise as a speaker or interested in becoming an author? We're calling all educators, innovators, and changemakers! Whether you're looking to publish your own book, contribute a chapter to one of our collaborative projects, or step onto the stage to inspire others, we want to hear from you. We offer both paid and visibility-boosting speaking opportunities, including free engagements designed to expand your reach and impact. To join our movement, connect with Dr. B today!

Simply scan the QR code below or click on the Bling QR code to get started on your journey with us.

References

Underwood, A. (2013). *Educators' Understanding of Poor Working Memory and Metacognition-Building Interventions to Create Effective Instructional Designs* (Doctoral dissertation). University of Phoenix.

Get to Know Dr. B

Dr. María Angélica Benavides, known as Dr. B., is the Ultimate Legacy Builder and the Founder of the Alive and Beautiful Foundation. A global private publisher with B-Global International Publishing and a visionary leader, Dr. B. empowers entrepreneurs, service providers, humanitarians, and survivors to transform their stories into impactful legacies. Her work centers on guiding individuals toward lasting influence and success through purposeful storytelling and strategic growth.

In addition to leading the Alive and Beautiful Foundation, Dr. B. serves as the Global Educational Reform Chairperson for Leaders of All Nations International. She is also the Founder of Unified MINDS Academy K-12 Online, supporting dropout students, the underprivileged, and the homeschool community. Through PowerTalk Productions and B-Global Magazines, Dr. B. hosts platforms dedicated to sharing stories globally, inspiring, and supporting humanitarians, business owners, and service providers in amplifying their messages.

Contact Me

Blinq
https://blinq.me/6XdEPTRPdsS5664TXbOl?bs=db

Conclusion

The Educational Luminaries: Triumphing Over Systemic Hurdles culminates in a powerful call to action. The insights and approaches presented here underscore the urgent need for a paradigm shift in how we perceive and deliver education. These luminaries demonstrate that transformative education goes beyond academic success; it equips students to be adaptive thinkers, compassionate leaders, and change-makers.

As we close this journey of exploring pioneering minds across disciplines, we are reminded that true educational reform requires not just the participation of educators but the collaboration of visionaries from all walks of life. By fostering diversity, equity, and inclusion, addressing trauma, integrating advanced technology, and bridging gaps in media literacy, we can create a system that prepares every student for a meaningful and impactful life.

Our journey toward revolutionizing education is ongoing. This book serves as both a guide and an invitation to embrace change, challenge norms, and create a future where education is a transformative, life-empowering experience for all. Let these luminaries inspire you to be part of this revolution, introduce bold ideas in your own communities, and help close the gaps that limit our potential to educate and empower. Together, we can make an indelible mark on the world through education.

Call to Action

As we conclude *The Educational Luminaries: Triumphing Over Systemic Hurdles*, we invite you to join us in taking these insights from inspiration to action. The journey toward a more inclusive, dynamic, and impactful educational system requires not only ideas but also the commitment to bring these ideas to life within our communities.

We offer specialized training programs designed to empower educators, administrators, and community leaders with the tools they need to lead effectively, inspire positive change, and cultivate a love for learning in their students. Our programs focus on developing leadership skills, enhancing reading and writing abilities, and guiding participants through the transformative process of writing a book by the end of the year—a powerful means to strengthen communication, boost self-confidence, and give voice to individual experiences.

In response to the pressing needs discussed in this book and the unique challenges faced by districts and schools, we also provide topic-based workshops and training sessions. These sessions cover a wide range of relevant areas, from integrating diversity, equity, and inclusion initiatives to addressing trauma in education, implementing media literacy, and exploring the role of artificial intelligence in modern pedagogy. Each topic is carefully crafted to align with the most current needs of educators and schools, ensuring that the training we provide is both timely and transformative.

We encourage you to reach out, participate, and share these opportunities with others in your community. Together, we can create a supportive network of educational leaders and innovators who are dedicated to shaping a brighter, more equitable future. Let us close the gaps, inspire a love for learning, and build an educational system that serves every student.

Join us in this mission—let's make an impact that will resonate for generations to come.

Get the Latest Updates!
- **SPEED NETWORKING**
- **PUBLISHING OPPORTUNITIES**
- **CONFERENCES & MASTERMINDS**
- **UPCOMING PUBLICATIONS**

Join the Mailing List

https://inspiringleaders.network/

JOIN US!
INNOVATIVE LEADERS DISRUPTING EDUCATION
FREE LinkedIn Group

https://bit.ly/ILDEgroup

Connect with us on LinkedIn:
www.linkedin.com/in/donnavallese
www.linkedin.com/in/drbglobal